Parracombe Prize 2022

short story competition

This anthology has been selected from entries to the Parracombe Prize 2022 short story competition, and it is dedicated to all the authors who entered.

ISBN 978-1-8384822-2-0

Published by Parracombe Community Trust

Results of the Parracombe Prize 2022

First prize
Alison Allen, *Growing Power*

Second prize
Fiona Thackeray, *Are We There Yet?*

Joint third
K A Bigelow, Many Happy Returns
Marcella Hourihane, *El Scorcho*

A further 31 stories were long-listed and are included in this anthology.

Contents

The Stoat

Her spade sliced into the earth. Her foot was on the tread and she pushed, hard. She kept the blade sharp so it cut cleanly into the soil. She leant on the handle to tilt it. A clod of dark earth came free. She lifted it out and laid it carefully on the undug ground. The hole was coming along. A foot square, twelve inches deep. She squatted down and, with a gloved hand, crumbled the damp, rich soil at the bottom. She couldn't feel it properly. She took off her gloves, dug into the raw earth with her broken fingernails, grasped a handful in her cupped hands and raised it to her face. She sniffed. She could almost taste the musty metallic scent of newly cut earth. It might not attract a Parisian perfumer, but she loved it. Why did they want to take it away from her?

She wanted to curl into the hole and stay there forever.

She sighed and shook her head. She needed to finish digging, to plant the hazel whip and move on to the next hole. A bundle of twenty stems lay on the ground. She wouldn't see the trees grow, put out their rough leaves, dangle their catkins, form their first nuts. It didn't matter. It didn't matter. She lifted the first thin stem into the hole. Threads of root branched away from the finger-thick tap like unruly hair. They had plenty of space. She had planned the hole perfectly. Holding the sapling, she scattered crumbled earth into the hole, careful not to crush; to support, not to break. She shook in more earth until the root was encased in a comfortable blanket of soil, and she could scrape the last clods onto the top. She stamped firmly with her boot all around the stem. The hazel was secure and safe. Planted.

Alice was a quiet woman. She was a watcher, a listener. Sometimes her workmates would forget she was even there.

Brought up on a farm tucked into the shadows of the Mendips, she had worked on the land all her life. She ran with the rhythms of seasons, sleeping early and long in the winter, alert and sleepless in summer. She lived alone now, after encounters with men that bewildered her and left her wary and guarded. She had worked on this particular land, in this particular wood, for nigh on ten years. Her hair had grown grey as she watched wood anemones spread from the first handful of bulbs planted under an oak tree. She watched the blackbird pair build their nest, year after year, in the same hawthorn, blue tits chatter and gather as they hid from the eyes of the sparrow hawk. She had stayed after nightfall, when she should have left the grounds, and listened to the hoot of the tawny owl. She'd watched the deer skitter out to drink from the pond and badgers shamble and snuffle along paths designed for human feet. The animals saw Alice. They weren't frightened. They were used to her. She was part of the wood.

It was all changing now. Since he had taken over. Alice called him the Stoat. It was his sleekness, his wide chest, his smooth hair. And his habits. When Alice was a little girl, she had watched a stoat one evening. She'd gone to collect eggs from her hens. A stoat had dug a hole under the fence into their enclosure. It was dancing, whirling, spinning, trying to catch its tail as the hens watched - fascinated, hypnotised. The stoat spun closer and closer until – it leapt. It tore their throats out, their blood spurting, staining its pure white chest red. Alice didn't stop it. She was mesmerised too. The Stoat, Alice's new boss, was the same. Staff would come back from meetings wide-eyed, talking of targets and evaluations, of flow charts, reviews and assessments. They all had to participate, they said. They all had to pull together. Alice would slide out. She'd place a hand on the grey bark of the oak for reassurance. Then she'd go back digging, pruning, staking, clearing, raking, planting just as she had always done. She'd look over the wood, and she'd know which tree suckers should be removed to create light and space, where the judicious removal of a rotting branch would save a whole tree, when to harvest the best elder flowers, where to find the juiciest blackberries, the only edible fungi. The life cycle of the wood flowed through her blood.

Alice dug the next hole. This time she was thinking of the Stoat. She jabbed at the soil viciously. It resisted. She wrestled with the spade as it clanged against a stone embedded deep in the ground; she wrenched at the earth, and it fought back. The hole she dug was pitiful, the sides collapsing, the edges ragged. She had tried to do as the Stoat asked. To fill in the forms, to write the weekly reviews; she really had tried. She picked up the next sapling. The words on the instruction label danced in front of her swimming eyes. She didn't need to be told. She knew how to plant a tree. She thrust the root into the hole and shovelled the earth onto it, stamping hard. When she stood back the sapling lurched at a strange angle.

'Ms Graham!' Alice heard her name. He was walking across the field towards her, picking his way through the cow pats in his city shoes, the grass wetting the bottoms of his trousers. He was waving.

Alice snapped the tip off the sapling. The wood was pale under the bark, the flesh white. A bud was sprouting on the side of the stem, pinkish in the grey. She flicked it off with her fingernail.

The Stoat was getting closer. He had neared the fence and was searching for a gate.

Alice took her knife from her pocket and started to whittle the sapling tip, slitting the bark away from the wood. The tip snapped. She moved further down, stripping the grey back to the palest green-white. Naked flesh damp with sap.

The Stoat scrambled over the fence, his jacket flapping. On the other side, Alice's side, he straightened his suit, smoothed his hair, adjusted his trousers. He found the path that led up the hill towards her.

Alice's knife sliced through the flesh of the sapling, swiping again and again to form a point.

'Ms Graham!' the Stoat said. 'There you are!'

'Afternoon,' she said.

'You didn't come to our meeting. So I've brought the meeting to you.'

'Yes, sir.'

'I shouldn't have to make a habit of doing that.'

'No, sir.'

'It's a waste of my time, you know.'

'I know, sir.' Alice shuffled her feet. The Stoat looked at the shaved bark, the naked destroyed sapling by her side. Alice followed his eyes.

'Don't know what came over me, sir. I'll pay for it, sir.'

'That won't be necessary.'

Alice knew why it wouldn't be necessary. She was for the chop. She was the old wood. They'd snap her off and sweep her away like a dead branch. She hung her head.

'Ms Graham, you've worked this wood for a long time. Would you care to tell me about it?'

So the Stoat wanted to know what she did. So she could be replaced. Alice started reluctantly. She told him about the hazels she was planting. To make an archway. How they would take fifteen years to grow to full height. How they could be coppiced to produce fine walking sticks and fencing. Then, she showed him where the sweeps of bluebells appeared in spring. She knelt down and lifted a leaf that flapped over a wren's nest. She flipped over a rotting log to make the insects that lived underneath scatter, and she made him raise his eyes to see the pair of buzzards swooping overhead. She hadn't spoken so much in years. He laughed. The words dried in her mouth.

'Very educational,' he said. She stared at him. He took a piece of paper out of his pocket.

'I wanted to ask, is this from you?' He showed her the paper. She could see that it was the form he'd asked for, a weekly review of their work. To include all procedures, problems and plans. It was the one that she had filled in.

'I thought that staff would use the computer.'

'I'm not much of a one for computers, sir,' she said.

'I can see that,' he said. She'd found a pencil stub in the shed and used that. She'd done her best.

She waited. It was coming, she knew.

The Stoat looked out over the wood.

'My sister has dyslexia,' he said. 'Struggled with it all her life, although there are things you can do these days, ways to learn. She has affinity with the wild, just like you.'

Alice didn't know what dyslexia was. What she had didn't have a name when she was little, and if it did it was just called thick, stupid and idle. She didn't need to read to work in the woods. Didn't need to write. Didn't want to use words.

The Stoat continued to stare out across the fields.

'I thought, maybe you could use this for your reviews. Just to let me know what's going on.' He handed her a small machine, not much bigger than a cigarette lighter.

'What's that?'

'A Dictaphone,' he said. He showed her how to press a button and record her voice, how to play it back. For the first time, Alice smiled.

'Once a week, tell me what you've been doing, like you did just now. What's happening in the wood, what's growing, what's not, wildlife, you know the kind of thing. Bring it back to the office. We could write it up as a blog. It might make you famous, you never know.'

Alice had no idea what he was talking about. But it looked like she wasn't going to lose her job.

The Stoat held out his hand. Alice took it in hers and shook it.

'Thank you,' she said, and she watched as he clambered back over the fence and picked his way back across the field to his office.

Don't Forget Your Dancing Shoes

They're not used to women my age having so much hair. They say, 'A nice pixie cut is what you want. It's much easier.' Easier for them, that means. But I've got an ally. He's one of the carers here, a sweet young man. 'Can I play with your hair?' he says. He likes brushing and styling it. He uses all the old combs and clips you gave me. He'll be here soon to do what he calls an *up do* because I said I wanted to look good tonight.

I've chosen your birthday. I want it to be a special day, but it can't be my own birthday because there's always a big fuss here. It would be too much in one day. Poor Charlotte had her 100th yesterday, and she's exhausted. They'd persuaded her to have her hair cut. Told her it would make her look younger. As if she cared! In fact, she does look younger now. She looks like a trusting child who's being tricked by older siblings. She had no idea what the cake and the singing and the presents were all about, nor who the mayor and all the usual suspects from local services were. But she smiles a lot, so it's easy to imagine she's enjoying herself.

I smile too, but mostly when I'm talking to you. I have to talk to you. Nobody else sees things the way you and I used to. I don't know anyone else who could remember that far back. They probably think I'm talking to myself. But they know I'm not like Charlotte. The other day, I heard someone say, 'Old Georgina's razor sharp, you know!' They've removed every other sharp item, but they've overlooked my brain.

I know you're there, somewhere. I can feel you. Your body gave up twenty years ago, but whatever else we're made of stayed behind. I bet you're hiding in one of the trees you loved, perhaps curled up in an old bird's nest. So, listen carefully, please. Listening was never your strong point, so I don't suppose you've changed. I want to tell you about the girls and our plan, so you can be ready. I don't want anything to go wrong.

In a little while, Tibor will come. He's the young carer I mentioned. He's from Budapest. He loved England when he first came, but he's not sure now if it's sensible to stay. He's been set upon more than once and told to *go back where he came from*. That reminds me of Mosley's thugs in the thirties. I thought we'd seen the last of all that ugliness, but perhaps it will always be with us, hiding away in some back alley, just waiting for the signal to rise up and catch us off our guard again. Tibor says he doesn't like the way politics are moving in Hungary either. When I told him what I thought about that referendum, he gave me a hug and said, it's a pity I wasn't the prime minister! He showed me how to spell his name and taught me how to say it. He was pleased that I wanted to get it right. To help me remember, I wrote down *tea* and *bore*. 'I won't forget those two words, living in a place like this,' I said. Tibor roared with laughter. The other carers would have been all stony-faced.

Where was I? Yes, Tibor will come, and he'll say, 'Hello George, how are you this evening?' The other staff use the name on my official documents, but he asked me what I preferred to be called, and I told him you'd always called me George. He asked if he could do the same. I liked that. Anyway, he'll come, supposedly to help me get ready for bed. But he said he'd love to put my hair up, if that's what I'd rather do. The others would tell me it's too late in the day for posh hairdos. But Tibor will do it. He knows I never want to go to bed early. I can manage to get undressed and into my nightclothes myself. Undoing things isn't as hard as doing them up. He understands I don't like spending all evening sitting in my dressing gown.

The next bit's more complicated. I've had time to think about it. I just hope I can do it. The night duty starts at eight o'clock. I'm usually still in the lounge then, which is right by the front door. They call me the night owl. I've noticed that each member of the afternoon team is paired with someone of the night team. It takes about ten minutes for them all to swap over. Once that's done, I should be able to slip out, while the night carers are all in the back office, checking up on what has been happening during the day and what needs to be done overnight. I don't know the code for the door, but I've learnt the position of each of the four buttons they press. That Pelmanism game the activity carer does with us is really useful!

I've chosen my favourite spot in the garden. It isn't far. It's nicely overgrown because nobody else goes there. I used to go by myself several times a day, when I could walk better. I'm supposed to have someone with me now, so I can only go when a carer is free. That isn't nearly often enough. But I should be able to get there with my stick. The birds love it. It must have been a splendid vegetable plot once, when this was a private house.

I'll head for the old stone seat. I'd like to sit there for a while, before the others arrive. I wonder if I'll still be able to pick up that heady scent of the honeysuckle just as the daylight fades. If I'm very quiet, I might be able to hear the foxes and badgers coming out. I used to see them regularly when I first came to live here. I don't hear so well now, but if the tawny owls are around, I'll hear them. In here, there's always too much noise from the televisions, and there are never enough windows open. I struggle to hear anything interesting from outside. I'd like to come across those beautiful creatures once more.

It's always too hot in here. I'll take my wrap, but the contrast with the cold outside will get to me before long. But that's all right. The girls said they'd bring a wheelchair and some blankets to keep me warm. They said they would meet me at the seat, and we'll all go round to the woods.

Now, let me tell you about the girls. They're a class act. You'll love them. One's called Julie and the other is Cathy, but I keep getting them the wrong way round, so I'll just call them 'the girls'. They're thirteen, and they've been visiting me in the garden. Their school is doing some sort of project about the oldest local residents they can find. They said I'm the star of the show because I was born just before the end of the First World War. I'm the oldest person in the village. The first time, they arrived looking all sheepish, as if they were expecting me to smell bad. When we started chatting, they asked me why I kept referring to it as the Great War, rather than the first one. 'What was great about it?' one of them had said.

'Nothing in any good way, but it was huge, so that's what everyone called it.' After a moment, I added, 'And we didn't know then, that there was going to be a second one.' Strangely, it was this young girl's question that brought that point home to me. At their age, I was never allowed to speak to old people, unless they spoke to me first. I'm glad young people can do that now.

They wanted to know if I had any memories of the war. 'No,' I said. 'I was too little.' Their faces dropped. 'But I do have something from just after the end.' They perked up. I told them about a penny, which I've still got in my bedside table.

'Wow!' they said. 'Can we see?'

I told them how it was given to me by my brother, Joe. Apparently, we were with our mum in a huge crowd, lining one of the main streets in Liverpool. Mum was carrying me, and we were waving goodbye to lots of men. Joe said he would never forget the tramp, tramp, tramp sound of their feet. Some years later, he told me they were American soldiers, marching down to the docks to get on boats to take them home. They were throwing their loose English change to the children. Joe caught one, then he caught another one, and he gave it to me.

After that, they asked me to describe as much as I could remember about home, when I was a child. They loved hearing about bath time. They thought I was joking, when I talked about heating up the water in what we called 'the copper', then filling up a bucket, going backwards and forwards, to take all the hot water to the bath. My brothers and I used to take it in turns, all in the same water. The girls thought that was bad enough. 'Hope you were allowed to go first,' they said. But they really screwed up their noses when I said, 'We did that only once a week.'

When we talked about birthdays, they were sweet enough to ask me what I would like to do for mine. I don't recall anyone here doing that, even when I had my big one with the greeting from the Queen. They were most put out, on my behalf, when I said that, as far as I knew, everything had already been arranged. We talked about what birthdays were like when I was young. 'We didn't have parties,' I said, 'but when we were little, we had days out to a beach. When we were your age, we had to make our own entertainment.' They were intrigued when I said that one of my best birthdays, with my brothers and some of our friends, was a picnic in the woods after dark. I told them I had always loved animals, and that's the best time to come across many of them. The girls were amazed I was allowed to do that. They went into a little huddle, fussing with their phones and giggling. I thought they were being rather rude, but after a few minutes, one of them said, 'Are you up for an evening picnic? You could have an official birthday on a different day. The Queen does it, so why shouldn't you? We can sort that for you with our friends.'

I was so delighted, I clapped my hands. But I could see problems straight away. 'I wouldn't be allowed to go out by myself, and they wouldn't allow you to be in charge of me,' I said. 'You're too young.'

They thought for a moment, and then the other one said, 'We're not planning to tell them. Are you?' When I laughed, she said, 'Let's keep it a secret. The difficult bit will be you getting out.'

So, that's up to me. Fingers crossed!

Ah! I can hear Tibor coming. I've got butterflies, like the first time you asked me to dance. But that worked out all right, didn't it? Bring a bottle of Malbec, will you? For Charlotte's do, we were given some fizzy stuff that smelled like disinfectant. I'd love a decent drink. The girls said they'll bring some *old people's music.* They probably mean from when their parents were young, but you never know. Do you think we could still manage a foxtrot? Please come. I'd love you to meet the girls. I've talked to them about things that even you didn't know.

And don't forget your dancing shoes.

Karth8

The red, all-seeing eye of the scanner casts out its rays, capturing the white boxes and mutant animal shapes sealed away in their containers. Karth8 swore under his breath. Meal-times in the mines of Moria was a necessary evil. His choices were limited. Either his captors would force him to eat again, or he would have to escape.

The machine's worshipping attendant, a plump humanoid popping with adolescence, sneered at Karth8. Fat, stubby fingers poked at the keyboard while his other hand pushed more packages towards the hero of three planets and one wobbly moon.

'Glibly boy now, glibly!' barked a familiar voice.

Glibly? The rap on Karth8's head ripped him out of one space-time continuum and into another.

'Ricky. *Help me.* Now!'

His mother's frustrated look drove Ricky to action. Grabbing from the pile of frozen food and disassembled chicken packs, he tossed them one after the other into their tote bag.

The checkout attendant rang up the last item. A pink bubble of chewing gum peeked out between his pursed lips before disappearing with a 'snap' as he handed Ricky's mom her receipt.

'Did you hear me?'

Her voice shrieked like claws scraping on a pane of glass. Karth8 wrapped his cloak of invisibility tighter. He was backed up against the dungeon's cold wall and could go no further. Luckily, the wooden ledge on which he lay was above the goblin's reach. He should be safe, but he held his breath too.

The bat-like ears of his tormentor were sensitive to the slightest sound.

The ledge vibrated. He'd been discovered! Karth8 peeked out from a fold as red-tipped claws reached for him. There was still one desperate measure to avoid being assimilated. Using three of the six fingers on his one hand, he invoked the Krilian blinding-flash spell. Before he could complete the intricate movements, one of her claws caught the collar of his thermal regulator and threatened to strangle him.

His big sister glared at him. 'It's dinner. Why do you make this so difficult?'

'*Glet, goh!*' Despite the similarity to the Yarvish phrase, 'Golly gosh,' it wasn't what he was trying to say.

Coughing, he tried again. '*Let go!*'

She relaxed her grip, but didn't release him as if uncertain of his intentions. With her other hand, she yanked off the blanket.

Her face scrunched in a frown. 'It's Thursday. You know what that means. Mom wants you down for dinner. Pronto!'

Her bugged-out eyes and thin lips reminded him of one of his least favourite Darthkin slave-masters. Darthkins were famously thin-skinned and easily riled; he'd almost lost a finger escaping from them. Which would have been awful – he didn't want to be confused with a human.

'OK.'

'Don't *OK* me.' She tugged at his T-shirt. 'Get. Out of bed. Now.'

His eyes bored into hers. His brow knitted in concentration, and his voice dropped as he used the Force. 'You will tell Mom you couldn't find me…'

She shook her head and released him.

It worked! There was a first time for everything. This would make things much easier…

'You're just making it harder on Mom, you know.' Her face disappeared from the top bunk, and the bedroom door slammed shut.

The inter-dimensional prison wagon slid into a berth, and the doors popped open. Karth8 didn't move; he was slumped over staring at his kneecaps. His legs felt like blocks of concrete and weren't responding to commands. He really should have replaced them with an upgraded version, probably something powered by an arc reactor. Next overhaul he would do it.

His mother sighed. 'Ricky. Please get out of the car.'

She held the door open, her face a mixture of frustration and sympathy. As long as she wasn't sad; that was always worse. There was no hiding then.

Ricky followed his sister and mother into the building and rode up in the elevator. He wrinkled his nose at the smell of antiseptic wipes and mystery treatments. The elevator 'dinged' open and they entered a long corridor. The pastel green and yellow hallway seemed a sanctuary, as what happened behind the many doors branching from it was anything but.

Ricky stood alone at the head of the bed. He snuck his small hand under his father's limp one. White tape secured a needle and tube inserted into the skin on top of his dad's hand. Fluids with dyslexic names dripped from bottles and plastic bags suspended above the bed.

This time Karth8 would succeed, he was sure of it. For months he had made the ritual visit and tried all the techniques he could research to bring his overlord back to his family's space-time. Nothing had worked.

He studied the figure before him. Long locks of brown hair had been swept away from the drawn face. Dark stubble hinted a shave was due. One cheek was decorated with the faint red imprint of lipstick from his mother or his sister. The hazel eyes were shut, the ones that used to read him stories of far-off worlds. That was all gone. For months, his overlord had been cast down by some devilry. Nothing could open those eyes, not even a Yarvish mind-jolt. He'd tried that.

Karth8 knew he had only minutes before his keepers

returned. The solution was obvious now. How could he have not tried this before? He closed his eyes and focused on the hand on top of his; the warmth, the security of it. He spoke the three holy words of the Netherene soul-casters to temporarily boost his brain. Screwing his face up with the effort, he shouted with his mind, *Dad, where are you? Give me a signal. I'll come to you.*

A finger on a five-fingered hand twitched.

All the Things You Aren't

Bob was one of the few people in the entire western world who hated the Beatles. It was personal: they'd completely fucked him and his generation, was the way he saw it.

Bob played the saxophone. It was jazzers like him who'd been sunk by the tidal wave of pop music. They should have seen it coming, he and Tubby and the others. They kept hoping that their music would win through. Wasn't jazz the greatest music of the twentieth century? But the gigs gradually dried up after *She Loves You*. As the holes in his diary grew bigger, he remembered asking himself if this shitty pop music really could be the future. Now he had the answer. Three chords and a banal lyric could net you a fortune while, just to pay the bills, he was on yet another scruffy train.

Outside the train window a grey drizzle wafted past. The fields were slabs of glistening mud, pocked with soupy puddles. Somewhere up the line ahead he'd be prostituting his talent at yet another one-nighter. Gazing out, he could faintly see his reflection in the train window. Hair sleeked back. Moustache limply hanging on his top lip. Eyes hinting at insomnia.

Everyone agreed he was talented. A year or two before *Jailhouse Rock*, one of the magazines had called him, "the English Dexter Gordon". That'd pissed him off. He was Glaswegian, for fuck sake! Three or four years later, he'd released *A View From The Bridge*, with a cover featuring him and Tubby Wickham standing on Tower Bridge trying and, he had long ago admitted, failing to look like Chet Baker and Gerry Mulligan. 'More like fuckin' Laurel and Hardy,' Tubby'd said. Reviewing the album, another magazine had voted him best newcomer. Newcomer? He was nearly thirty! A lot of the jazz greats were dead by thirty.

Journalists: all arseholes.

Some days he tried to focus on the better times. He nearly played with Miles Davis once. Miles had heard *A View From The Bridge*. He'd phoned Bob from Paris.

'French Cat's got problems with his chops,' Miles growled. 'C'nyou giddout 'ere?'

Bob would have been on the next plane. Only Miles' agent phoned back later to say the "French Cat" was okay after all.

'You miserable git,' Tubby had ripped into him as they drove to a gig shortly afterwards. 'Sittin' there wallowing in sorrow. At least he fuckin' asked you. The only fucker who asks me is you.'

By the time the train crawled into the station, the drizzle had turned to heavy rain. He waited for a cab, squinting through the gloom up the wet strip of road for any sign of incoming taxis. He thought about Tubby. Tubby had escaped all this. He'd drowned himself in booze. For some it had been heroin. Bob and Tubby had both chanced their arms with that, but each had managed to pull out of the nose-dive before fatal impact. They fled to whisky and beer. Lots of it. In Tubby's case, enough to turn his liver to leather. The cirrhosis made him weak, a dose of pneumonia finished the job. He was forty-two.

Sometimes Bob played along to Tubby's records. Maggie hated that. 'Just let him go, for Christ sake,' she'd said once. She left him shortly afterwards. Went off with a drummer from Burnham-on-Crouch. Bob knew what Tubby would have said. 'It's always the fuckin' drummer.' Now he played the records louder and for longer. He wove his solos round Tubby's horn which was doomed to play the same notes in the same order forever. The ultimate cruelty for a jazzer.

'Let me guess - Butlin's?' the cab driver chirped.

Not Birdland. Not The Bluenote. Note even Ronnie's. 'Yeah. Billy-bloody-Butlin's, mate,' Bob sighed.

The plaster on the over-sized stucco entrance arch to the camp was blown in a few places, and the "u" of Butlin's had fallen off. On a hoarding on the left pillar was last year's poster for "Miss Butlin 1966", faded to washed-out blues and pinks. Looking at the dreary exterior, Bob couldn't help think that what the Beatles had done for jazz, cheap flights to Spain had done for Butlin's. Those Technicolour adverts from the 1950s, with well-toned young men, jack-knifing from high boards into azure pools filled with slim, laughing women, all basking in an everlasting golden summer, had given way to peeling paint and the smell of chip fat in the cavernous dining halls.

A man in a tacky red greatcoat covered in gold braid was slumped in a glass booth at the entrance.

'You with the band?'

'Yeah.'

'Straight down past the pool, right at Funland, and the ballroom's in front of you.'

Tonight Bob would be playing with The Highliners, the next in a long line of local rhythm sections who would struggle to keep up with him. He wandered into the ballroom where a drummer was whacking experimentally at a battered kit. To his left, a very long, thin pianist was peering through his fringe at a tangle of leads.

As Bob opened his sax case, the drummer, who'd stopped thrashing, walked over to welcome their guest player.

'Alright Bob? It's a real honour to play with you. I'm Spike.'

'Thanks Spike. How do you know me then?'

'I've got that great album you done what was voted best newcomer. Lovely playing. Still one of me favourites.'

'Well that's nice. I don't get noticed much these days.'

'That's so crap man. You used to be one of the British greats.'

Spike ushered Bob to the bar and insisted on buying the drinks. Three pints and three generous double whiskies had gone down by the time the long, thin pianist summoned Spike and Bob for a sound check.

The barman handed Bob a double-cum-triple whisky. 'Take one up on the stand mate.' Bob smiled, looking intently at the barman, who seemed to be blurring just slightly. He walked back with Spike, being very careful where he placed each foot. When he bent down to get his horn out, the floor lurched, and he had to steady himself with both hands on the sax case for a few seconds. A shower of tiny light spots drifted round the room off the glitter ball. The room also seemed to move in the same direction as the light spots. Concentrating very hard, he picked up the sheaf of music, the standards they'd play that night, and walked slowly towards the microphone. It was 8 o'clock. He looked round the room. It was mostly empty chairs. Bob counted seven people dotted around. Sitting alone in the front row was a woman in her fifties trying to look twenty-five. A few more stood at the bar, just beyond his focus. Tubby would have called it, "man-to-man marking".

The pianist mumbled, 'Whenever you like.'

Bob coughed.

'Thank you for coming tonight, ladies and gentlemen.' He fiddled with the mouthpiece. 'I'm Bob Welford.' He paused again, snorted air through his nose. 'I used to be a British great.' He looked intently at the chart on the music stand. 'We're going to start tonight with a tune that's been covered by everyone worth knowing - *All The Things You Are.*'

Spike and the bass player kicked in together, and the pianist noodled the opening chords over them. Bob put the sax to his mouth and sucked at the reed. He stared intently at the octave key on the neck of his instrument then raised his eyes to where an audience should have been.

He took the sax away from his mouth. The rhythm section kept going, waiting for the horn. In his head Bob played with the title: *All the things you used to be. Things ain't what they used to be. All the things you aren't.* After the first thirty-two bars the pianist, looking desperately at Bob to no avail, had begun to solo. Bob stared out at the seven people. He looked up at the glitter ball. He fingered a key or two on the instrument. The pianist continued his solo into the next 32 bar sequence. And Bob realised this was it. This was where The Beatles had led him.

He unhooked the sax from its strap, turned his back on the audience and walked over to the chair. He took the mouthpiece off the sax and put them both in their case, leaned it against the drum-riser and walked off stage.

Outside the steady rain had thinned to drizzle. One battered red minicab was waiting by the rank at the camp entrance. Bob got in and asked for the station. On the train back, all he could see out of the window was the orange glow of the sodium lamps on the main road that tracked the railway along its course back to London. He felt unusually calm. About half an hour into the journey, he started to imagine what an obituary might say about him. Tubby had only merited a few cursory lines in the *Melody Maker.* But Tubby had died while he was still working. Having stepped off the bandstand for good, no one would remember Bob in another ten or fifteen years. The idea of an obituary to himself, however, appealed to him. He began to compose fragments in his head:

The death has been announced of the British jazz saxophonist, Robert Welford.

Or would they make the usual mistake and call him "English"? And if they did, who'd be left to point out the cultural faux pas? And would they consign him to a nailed-on "used to be" status?

> 'He is best known for his 1957 album *A View From The Bridge* that featured his long-term collaborator, Eric "Tubby" Wickham on trumpet. The record brought his playing to the attention of Miles Davis, who was in France recording *Lift to the Scaffold.* Davis had originally hired French tenor player, Barney Wilen, to work with him, but Wilen developed a painful gum infection a week before the recording date. Welford was contacted by Davis to step in, but the Frenchman recovered and was able to fill the saxophone role. The album went on to become one

of the most famous in the jazz canon.'

That would be it of course. He'd be remembered for what had nearly happened rather than all the things he'd been. Even in death he'd still be "the nearly man".
More sodium lights flowed by. Finally, a slight smile flitted beneath the moustache. This was his version of a fictional obituary. He could write what he liked.

> 'Welford had been inactive for some years, but shortly before his death, he released a compilation album of some of his work called *Beyond The Bridge*. It sold remarkably well and is considered to have been a contributor to the renewed interest in jazz music that is sweeping the country. Sales of the record have pushed it into the album charts where it has reached a high of number three.'

Searching for a closing coda, he decided he'd use the quotation from Miles Davis: "Bob Welford was the best tenor player I never had".

Outside the muddy fields drifted passed to the accompaniment of a dreary 4/4 rhythm beaten out by the train wheels, carrying Bob to the end of the line.

The Yellow Man

Each evening, I would watch and wait, my eyes fixed on the highest point of the steep, cobbled street that flowed from the volcano's crater above me to the harbour below. As the monastery bell tolled six, the Yellow Man would appear.

In those days, there were two of them, for my father and uncle mined sulphur together. As he reached the front door, I would throw it wide and call to my mother, 'Papa is home!' This was her cue to open the back door; a simple routine that meant he could enter the house and, by keeping to the passageway that ran its length, reach the garden without having to touch anything. The sulphur mine had given our family a comfortable existence, but my mother hated the yellow powder that clung to everything it alighted upon. My father teased her, pretending to embrace me until a warning cry from the kitchen would be enough to send him scurrying along the corridor like a whipped boy. He made his way to the far end of the garden, where a flight of twelve steps had been cut into the cliff face. I watched his yellow head disappear from view and listened as he swam in the warm waters of the Aegean. As he bathed, he filled his lungs with air, heavy with the scent of sweet myrtle and pungent rosemary, and sang the folk songs he had learned in his youth. My mother placed clean clothes on the top step so that he could return to the kitchen, free from any trace of the 'Monster' as she called the volcano. As we ate, we shared our stories of the day: I told classroom tales, such as how the principal had sent me to fetch Father Leandros because Nico had insulted the icon of St. Simon the Apostle - although no one was quite sure what he had said. My mother related the gossip she had picked up at the market stalls, unpacking them like a basketful of tasty morsels. However, when it was my father's turn, he took great care never to mention the Monster but would tell of a bird's nest near the pathway, or how the flowers and trees were changing with the seasons. It was often my mother, who living in a state of constant fear for our safety, questioned him.

'Graciela says that there were rumblings yesterday.'

My father, trying to hide his irritation with his sister-in-law's loose tongue, would make light of it.

'It was nothing. Old Stefan's stomach rumbled louder than that during the priest's sermon last Sunday!'

My father always reminded her that no one had ever been killed by the volcano, but she would reply that the Monster had swallowed Theodore Bakirtzis. It was one of her convenient half-truths, for even the village children knew that Theodore had not gone to the volcano on the day of his disappearance. Instead, he had walked to the harbour, where he had taken passage to Kos and was swallowed, not by the Monster, but by the welcoming bosom of a young widow. My mother's fears became my fears. I was so tormented by nightmares after one visit, that further trips to the crater were forbidden. For weeks, vivid images of the sulphur-edged steam vents, which pockmarked the vast, barren caldera, troubled my sleep. I imagined that I was being smothered by the soft plumes of yellow gas that rose from its surface, sending a rotten egg stink skywards.

This was the only cause of disagreement in an otherwise happy marriage. My father regarded the volcano as the island's bounty; my mother, its curse.

The rhythm of our lives flowed on serenely, with barely a ripple disturbing its steady course until it changed in a single heartbeat. As soon as I reached the house that afternoon, I knew that something was wrong. When I entered the kitchen, I saw that my aunt and uncle were standing near to the table, while Father Leandros was seated opposite my father who, still coated in sulphur dust, sat in silence. His unwavering gaze was fixed on his yellow hands, and the powder that covered his face had been riven by a silent stream of tears that continued to flow, unabated. Suddenly, I realised that one person was absent from the group - my mother.

It was my uncle who finally gathered the courage to say, 'Mama...,' he faltered, and then realising that there was no easy way to tell me, blurted out, 'Mama died today!'

Piece by piece, the story was told. My mother had decided that it was only a matter of time before the volcano erupted, so each day, after my father had left for work and I for school, she would secretly take the boat out and practise rowing, little knowing that a childhood illness had weakened her heart. That morning when shopping in the market with Aunt Graciela, she had suddenly fallen to the ground. Doctor Aesculapius was called but could do nothing.

Gone in a single heartbeat.

For the next two years, our lives continued to follow a steady rhythm, although the melody had greatly changed. Just as the people of the island, sensitive to the feelings of Mrs Theodore Bakirtzis called her a 'widow' rather than an 'abandoned wife', so I became a daughter of the community and never a motherless child. Our village had many young widows who, having been denied the opportunity of motherhood by the war, now devoted themselves to my care. As I waited for sleep each night, the memory of my mother's face merged with that of others: pretty Sophia, who braided my hair with turquoise ribbons; gentle Eliana the farmer's wife, who gave me a kitten for company; and Aunt Graciela who, plagued by guilt that she was in some way responsible for my mother's death, took on many of our housekeeping duties. Each evening on my return from school, I would find a pot by the front door: rich moussaka in Eliana's brown, earthenware pot; exotic or colourful spiced vegetables in Sophia's blue, glazed dish. When a red, terracotta tagine waited patiently for my return, I embraced it joyfully and carried it to the kitchen with mounting anticipation, for it contained my aunt's specialty - an aromatic lamb stew, infused with fragrant spices and plump apricots. While I finished preparing our meal, my father followed his familiar bathing routine, but although I listened each evening, I heard nothing more than the lapping of the sea and the song of the woodlark in the myrtle tree above. Music had left his heart in a single heartbeat and silence, so loud that it pricked my ears, became the sound of our home.

Each Sunday, having put on our best clothes, we climbed the cobbled street to the heat-cupped courtyard simmering in the open glare. There, the Church of St. Simon the Apostle stood, rendered white, its sun-bleached walls beating back the midday sun. After the service, Althaia Makris would invite us to share a meal at her home. She lived in the largest villa on the island, perched high above the blue of the Aegean Sea. She and my father would sit on the terrace, sipping wine long into the balmy, Mediterranean twilight, while I was given free rein of the villa's library. As a young woman, Althaia had attended the university in Athens. While there, she had married Professor Makris, a famous surgeon, who had become wealthy by keeping the faces of the rich and famous forever young. He had built the villa, leaving his young widow well provided for. The library was filled from floor to ceiling with books, heavy with knowledge from every field of science. It was there that I could feed my insatiable desire to learn about anatomy and medicine.

One evening, shortly after my sixteenth birthday, three visitors arrived at our home: Father Leandros, Principal Tavoularis and Doctor Aesculapius came, like three wise men bearing gifts. Principal Travoularis spoke first. 'We have reached a point where our little school can offer you no more.'

I had been puzzled when, on the previous day, he had asked me what I would like to do in life. I had considered my friends: most of the boys became fishermen, farmers or builders, and most of the girls became the wives of fishermen, farmers or builders.

Doctor Aesculapius continued. 'I am not a young man and will not be able to serve the island for many more years.'

As I looked from one to another, trying to understand where the conversation was leading, Father Leandros spoke. 'The people of our island will need a new doctor in the future, and Mrs Makris tells me that you have a natural interest in medicine. We would ask you to consider training as a doctor. It would mean going to Athens to the Lyceum and then, if you do well, to the Medical School at the University of Athens.'

Each man's eyes were fixed on me, except for my father's, which seemed to be focused on a point somewhere near his shoes.

'Papa, is this your wish?' I asked.

His eyes brimmed with tears, and his voice cracked as he answered, 'Mama would have been so proud.'

Mrs Makris' sister was married to a professor at the Medical School in Athens and would be pleased to provide both accommodation and guidance. I also learned that Mrs Makris covered all of my expenses throughout the two years at the Lyceum and the six of medical training. And so, my life-course was set, and although I was excited as I embarked on my great adventure, my joy was tempered by concerns for my father's welfare. He took great pains to assure me that Aunt Graciela would keep him in order, and the years would pass, all too quickly.

As I had never left the island, it was agreed that Mrs Makris would accompany me to Athens and introduce me to her sister. The city proved to be full of excitement, especially for a child who had led a sheltered life and, as my father had said, the years passed all too quickly. I was happy there, but by the time my training was complete, I was ready to return home.

It had been arranged that I was to serve an internship with Doctor Aesculapius, working alongside him until his retirement. I disembarked at the harbour one afternoon in late summer and made my way home. Although my father was expecting my return, I had not told him the exact date.

I watched and waited, and as the monastery bell tolled six, the Yellow Man appeared. He made his way down the street, more slowly than I remembered. As he reached the door, I threw it wide and watched as the initial look of shock was quickly replaced by a wide smile that spread across his face, creating deep, yellow ridges and furrows in the sulphur powder that clung to him. For a moment, he raised his arms, as if to embrace me. The late afternoon sun glowed golden on his skin, but unlike King Midas, he stopped as the memory of my mother's voice brought a smile to his face.

'It's good to have you home.'

I watched as he went to the stone steps that led down to the warm waters of the Aegean. On the top step, he paused for a moment and gazed skywards. His eyes shone like the sun on the waves below, and his fine silver hair flew here and there like the wispy cirrus high above.

As I laid the table for our meal, a sound caught my ear. Faint at first, but growing in strength; it was my father's pure, clear voice.

Above him, in the gently swaying branches of the myrtle, a single woodlark piped a duet.

Playing Safe

The trumpet was singing, and the tuba was blurting out fat-bottomed notes like whoopee cushions. Roisin could feel Jacko's excitement building with the music until she thought he must burst.

'Isn't it just great, Mammy?' he whispered, never taking his eyes from the players as they reached the finale.

Roisin patted his leg but didn't reply. She was afraid of breaking the spell, even while she kept a lid on her hope. She'd never expected him to react like this. When she'd first suggested they came to the concert, he'd been less than enthusiastic. 'Square,' he'd grumbled. 'Who listens to the old tunes these days?'

Kids his age liked these new bands – *groups*, they called themselves now - with odd names. *Beatles. Rolling Stones. The Kinks.* What sort of names were those?

But she was grateful for anything that would break through the shell he had constructed around himself since his da had gone.

Jacko was an island of silence amid the chattering folk who streamed into the night after the last notes had faded away. He said nothing while they waited for the bus, and stared wordlessly past the reflected brightness of the window to the dark fields beyond, as they jolted down the lanes back to their village.

Roisin knew better than to press him. Her patience received its reward when she set a steaming cup of cocoa on the fender by his foot.

'Drink that up, and then it's away to your bed.'

He dragged his thoughts back from wherever they'd been.

'That was a grand sound, so it was. How long do you think it takes to learn to make sounds like that?'

She was going to say *a long time, son*, but something stopped her.

'You'll be going up to the new school in September, when you turn eleven. If they've a band, you could learn to play. What sort of instrument would you like?'

She prayed it would be something that wouldn't cost the earth. It was hard enough making ends meet as it was.

He turned shining eyes on her. 'Could I play the tuba?'

'We'll see.' The fail-safe for all occasions. 'Let's get you settled first.'

Holy Mother of God, let me be able to do this one thing for him.

Mr McCafferty wasn't sure that Jacko would be able to manage a tuba.

'The wee lad would be best starting on something simpler, Mrs Kinty. Sure, the instrument's bigger than he is,' he told Roisin.

But Jacko's eyes were so full of disappointment that he relented.

'Well, well, there's no substitute for enthusiasm. If the passion's there, that's half the battle. We'll see how you go, lad. First lesson on Friday.'

Day by day, Roisin watched Jacko coming back to life as he learned to master the piece of coiled brass. Her joy was diluted by apprehension. How was she ever going to afford to buy him one of his own? But for the time being, Jacko was happy to play the school tuba, dinted and scuffed as it was, and lug it backwards and forwards on the bus when he needed to practise at home.

It was a good job she had understanding neighbours. Roisin heard the oom-pah-pah issuing from Jacko's bedroom as she returned, bone weary, from her second job. It was getting late. Jacko should really be in bed. If he didn't stop in a moment, she'd have to go up and insist he give it a rest.

Silence fell as she made herself a cup of tea and a sandwich, but when she opened the door to his bedroom, there was a hasty scuffling. The tuba lay on the bed, and Jacko was looking suspiciously innocent, with a halo of smoke around his head.

Roisin sniffed the air. 'All right, where'd you get the cigarette, son?'

He let out his breath on a cloud of tobacco. 'Connor gave it me.'

'And how would Connor O'Rourke be getting so many ciggies he can start giving them away?' she demanded.

Jacko looked uneasy. 'He asks Mrs Lynch for a packet every time he goes into the shop.'

And she gives it to him. Connor's da was a big man in the Provos. The shopkeeper would be sure to keep on his good side, Roisin thought with a surge of panic, hearing the slight note of – what was it in her son's voice - Pride? Envy? Defiance?

'What have you to do with Connor? He's not in your year, nor is he in the band.'

He looked down. 'He's just someone at school. He takes me with him sometimes, when he goes to the shop, that's all.'

'Does Mrs Lynch give you ciggies as well?' She made her voice neutral.

Jacko looked up, radiating indignation. 'No.'

That was definite enough. Roisin started to relax, but a second glance at Jacko's face as he dropped his eyes had her knotting her eyebrows in a frown.

'But?'

He hunched his shoulder, picking at a loose thread on the counterpane. 'She sometimes gives me a bar of chocolate if Connor's there.'

'You're not to take it,' Roisin said, taking him by the chin to force him to look at her. 'If I hear you're taking stuff off people, I'll have that tuba away from you.'

'Mammy! You wouldn't!'

'Try me,' she said.

It had been what she was afraid of when Jacko left the tiny junior school in the village for the big secondary in the town. Suppose he became one of the lads who roamed the streets looking for trouble.

They were too near the North and its bombs and bullets for her comfort, throwing stones at nervous young soldiers, who would shoot first and ask questions afterwards, was a dangerous trick, so it was.

When she was a child, folk would have cuffed your ear and told your ma on you. Now they'd shut their eyes and their doors and pretend not to see. And who could blame them, after that wee boy was shot because the men in balaclavas thought he was an informer? It was no comfort to you when you were dead that you'd merely been in the wrong place at the wrong time.

She didn't want Jacko mixing with the likes of Connor O'Rourke. She could only hope that his burgeoning love of music would save him from becoming sucked into the ambit of those for whom violence was fast becoming the norm.

The first few times she saw bruises on him, she accepted his explanation that he'd fallen playing football, or been clattered with a hurley, or walked into a door. It happened. She had a bruise, faded to jaundice now, on the side of her own face where she'd turned into a cupboard door left carelessly open. It happened, didn't it? But it was happening too frequently for it all to be accidental. She would have to do something; she couldn't let her son put his fingers in the trap that had caught his father.

If she went up to the school, made a fuss, wouldn't that just make things worse for him? She'd have to let things go on the way they were for the moment while, little by little, she made her plans, her arrangements.

She only hoped she would be in time.

Roisin heard Jacko push his way through the front door and emerged from the kitchen, wiping her hands on the tea-towel.

'You're late. I've the dinner in the oven, drying to a crisp. Where've you been?'

'Rehearsal. I'll just be taking this up to my room.' He hefted the tuba case, but Roisin pointed irritably to the corner of the tiny kitchen.

'Oh, leave it there. Come and wash. Your tea's spoiling.'

He hesitated, then put the case down with care and rinsed his hands under the tap. She set the meal on the table and pulled out her chair. The tuba case was in the way. Bending down to move it, she looked up with a grin.

'Jesus God! You'll be getting arms like a navvy, carting this thing about the place. What've you got in here – a body?'

The frozen expression on his face almost stopped her heart. She blinked, then heaved the tuba case onto the table.

'No, Mammy!' he cried, scraping his chair backward. 'Don't! Leave it!'

She clicked the catches and opened the case. At first glance, the tuba looked as normal, nestling in the tuba-shaped hole, but as she lifted it out, she could see the bell-like end had a package stuffed within it.

'Don't touch it!' Jacko's face was white. 'I've to take it to Mr O'Rourke.'

Roisin snatched up a pair of gardening gloves and eased the package from the instrument. Wrapped in grey plastic sheeting, it felt heavy for its size and curiously pliable. She knew exactly what it was.

'How many times have you done this?' she asked, hearing her voice cool and calm and wondering why she wasn't screaming.

'A few,' he mumbled.

'Jacko, how could you?'

His face went from milk-white to scarlet in an instant. 'They said I had to, because of my da. They said he was an informer, and he went over the Border and got a bullet in his brain to pay him. I've to show them I'm not going the same road, or they'll put a bullet in mine. They will, Mammy.'

Roisin squeezed her eyes shut for an instant. She set the Semtex gently on the table and dropped the gloves on top of it. It was what she'd feared, since the day Alan went to the North and never returned, but she would grieve later.

'When does this have to get to O'Rourke?' she asked, nodding at the parcel.

'In the morning, before school,' he whispered.

'You'll take it to him. Then you'll come straight back here. I forgot to tell you, we're away on a wee holiday tomorrow.'

'A holiday?'

'Yes, but don't tell anyone. Not a soul, d'you hear? I'll get into trouble if they know I'm taking you out of school during term, but it's the only time I can have off,' she said, improvising wildly.

He looked at her with eyes wiser than an eleven-year-old's.

'Mammy, are we running away?'

Right this moment if we could, she thought, but she would not condemn them to spend their lives looking over their shoulders for the vengeance that would follow them if they did. There would be those who would curse her for allowing the death that Jacko carried to reach the men who would use it. But he was her son. She would keep him safe against the Devil himself.

'No, no. We'll just be away a couple of weeks,' she lied.

'Where will we go?'

Not America. She hadn't the money for the fares, and there were too many in America whose sympathies would lie with the O'Rourkes. And not London. The very plastic that sat in a lump on her table could reach them there.

'Yorkshire,' she said. 'We're going to Yorkshire. They've the wonderful bands there.'

His face brightened through the fear. 'Can I take my tuba?'

'We couldn't carry it with us, son, but we'll be back soon enough.' She saw he didn't believe her. 'And anyway,' she said, giving his shoulders a squeeze, 'it's time you had one of your own. We might find one in Yorkshire, and a band you can play it with.'

If she had to work her fingers to the bone, she'd get him a tuba. She was taking him away from all he knew, but his music would be a rock to keep him safe. The balaclavas had stolen her husband; she wouldn't let them have her son as well.

There must be nothing to tie the Semtex and Jacko together once it had left its hiding place. She put the gloves back on, carefully wiped fingerprints from the grey sheeting, then threw them in the bin. The gloves she'd buy in Yorkshire would only be used for gardening.

And the music Jacko would learn would not be songs of hate.

Here Is My Heart

The package arrived on Thursday. She carried the box into her apartment, examining it on all sides, but there was nothing to say where it had come from. Just a plain square box, neatly taped, with her name printed on the top.

Not even her address.

Just her name.

She took a steak knife to the seams, carving away the pristine flaps and hacking at the taped edges. She tilted the box on its side and dug through the Styrofoam peanuts until she located a squishy lump wrapped in several layers of tissue paper.

Beneath it sat a slightly damp note:

Here is my heart.

It's yours.

Please take care of it.

PS It likes peanut butter M&Ms

She stared at the note for a moment, then grunted and shrugged. 'That's odd.' She flicked the note on the floor and tore away the tissue paper.

There, in her hand, with bits of balloon-printed tissue paper stuck to its sides, was a human heart. It constricted and blood bubbled from the aorta.

'Well, that's lame.'

She dumped the heart in the box and forgot about it for a full day, but the heart continued to burble away nonetheless.

It woke her up at 3:17am, thumping and burbling until she swaggered into the kitchen.

'All right,' she said, her hair frizzed into a mane around her head. 'What do you want?'

The heart gurgled.

She put newspapers down in the laundry room and got an old blanket from the closet. When she set the heart on the blanket, it remained silent.

'Alright. Good night, then.'

As she turned to walk out of the laundry room, it burble-thump-gurgled.

She sighed and turned around with her hands on her hips.

'Do you know what time it is?'

The heart did nothing.

She tapped her foot on the linoleum, then went into the kitchen, filled a bowl of water, and brought it back into the laundry room.

'You're just going to have to deal with that until morning,' she said, shutting the laundry room door behind her. At least that way she wouldn't be able to hear its wheezy, slurpy noises.

The next day, she discovered the heart wasn't housetrained. Not only had it left her a little surprise in her favourite suede boots, but it had also managed to shred her favourite designer jeans and leave suspicious-looking stains all over the sofa cushions.

What she found behind the television, however, was the last straw.

She found the box it came in, stuffed whatever remained of the Styrofoam peanuts and shredded tissue paper back in, and dumped the heart inside. She wrapped tape all around the box and over every sliced-up seam. In big black marker, she scrawled, 'return to sender' across the top and set it out in front of her door.

When she came home from work, it was gone. Triumphant, she celebrated with a bottle of tequila and a phone call to the ex-before-last who kept next to nothing in his head, but knew his way around her bed well enough.

She deleted his number afterwards.

Two days later, the box returned.

Her neighbour across the way toddled over in a magenta muumuu. 'Oh, someone sent you a package! How lovely.'

A card on top said: *Sorry. No returns.*

'Yeah, it's fantastic.' She picked up the box and carried it to her kitchen.

She stood in the hallway and stared at it.

She watched *X Factor* with the volume turned up, so she couldn't hear it bumping against the cardboard.

She deleted seventeen friends from Facebook.

But the box was never far from sight.

Before she went to bed, she wedged it into her freezer between the fishless fingers and the Magnum bars.

A frozen heart was a quiet heart. Right?

During the night, the heart staged a break-out. It's unclear how it managed to escape the box, but the fishless fingers were used as levers to pry open the door.

The Magnums were nowhere to be seen.

Not only that, but it'd dirtied every dish and left them caked with dried food all over the apartment.

It left the toilet seat up.

On her way to work, she tossed it, box and all, into the nearest dumpster.

When she came home, it was lounging in her favourite chair watching reruns of *Project Runway*. She threw her bag on the couch and glared at it.

'Who gave you a key?'

A note taped to the TV said: *This is my heart. Take care of it.*

On Tuesday afternoon, she took the heart for a walk.

It started a fight with a Great Dane and tried to hump three Pomeranians.

They were firmly asked to leave after it relieved itself in a woman's purse.

On Wednesday, she decided they had to Have-A-Talk. She took it to a quiet café and made small-talk over lattes. She asked it what plans it had for the future, and when it shrugged apathetically, she demanded, 'Don't you want to do anything?'

It shrugged and said it was still finding itself, but there were a few things it might try.

She got fed up and stormed off.

The heart came back late. And drunk.

She locked it in the laundry room.

It gurgled and thumped at her all night.

The next morning, she mailed it to the ex-before-the-ex-before-last (whose number she deleted and sorely regretted).

He appreciated weird shit.

It came back, *Address Unknown.*

Beneath which had been typed: *This is my heart. Please take care of it.*

She knelt on the kitchen floor with the box in front of her and cried.

The heart gurgled.

'I don't want to take care of you!'

She threw the heart against a wall, and as it dripped down the white plaster, she had an idea. Armed with her trusty steak knife, she retrieved the heart and rinsed it off in the sink. With the precise attention only desperation brings, she halved and quartered it, then sliced it into narrow strips while she sautéed chopped onions and garlic in a pan. She scraped the heart-slivers into the pan with barbecue sauce and Burgundy wine. As it sizzled and browned, she smiled.

That night she slept better than ever before.

The next morning, there was a box outside her apartment door. Just a plain, square box with her name printed on the outside. Nestled on top of the Styrofoam peanuts was a note that read:

Here is my heart.

It's yours.

Please take care of it.

PS It likes peanut butter M&Ms

The Knife

I need a better simile.

A what?

A better simile. I have put, 'the knife went through her skin like butter'.

And what's wrong with that?

Too clichéd. Need something better.

I hear the corner kitchen cupboard door slam. God, how many more times? It's damp in that corner. Leave the God damn door open.

Leave the cupboard door open. It's damp, remember?

I hear him deliberately, very deliberately, open it - a notch.

What do you need a simile for anyway?

For this short story competition. I can write about anything, but then I had this dream about someone getting stabbed and I thought, great idea, will use that. Trying to organise the plot, work out who did it. Thought I'd start with the murder. But it's just not coming together.

I hear the kettle click on in response. Does he ever listen?

And what do you think about the way I am managing speech?

What?

Speech. I have seen this done in a few books recently. They simply ignore the speech marks.

Then how does the reader...?

They just work it out: tone, elliptical sentence structure, pronouns, colloquialisms, punctuation, speaker tags, paragraphing - that sort of thing.

'I prefer it the other way.'

I ignore him. Always negative.

What you cooking for lunch? - I ask.

Tomatoes on toast with balsamic vinegar.

Take the skins off the tomatoes.

But they are small tomatoes!!

Now look what you've made me do.

What?

You've made me use two exclamation marks. I hate using two exclamation marks.

But they're small tomatoes!

That's better. See, no need to shout.

I hear the rattle of cutlery in the drawer. Always rattling and rummaging. And then out comes the frying pan. He is using the wrong frying pan. I can tell by the noise it makes on the hob.

Are you using the right frying pan?

Didn't know there was a wrong one.

I ignore him and continue with my story. God, this is hard. I try to imagine the setting in a little more detail. Pathetic fallacy will do the trick.

I'm going to use pathetic fallacy - I say.

You what?

Pathetic fallacy: turn the weather into a metaphor – create a bit of mood. Make it rain, perhaps some flashes and rumbles.

No, don't do that, if you could just wait...

Outside rain splashed and streaked the panes.

What did you do that for? I was just about to hang out the washing - he says.

I ignore him, inspired now.

And maybe make it night time – murders are best served at night.

Outside, the rain continued and darkness fell.

What you doing? I wanted to go to Screwfix to get a new hedge-trimmer. Now they will be shut.

He wasn't happy - probably in a strop.

The clutter and batter of pans and plates spill from the kitchen and then, with a flourish of mood, he slams and slops a plate of tomatoes on toast, with balsamic dressing, in front of me. It smells very nice - but hardly an evening meal.

For dinner? Tomatoes on toast? - I say.

Well, it was daytime when I started cooking – and dry.

He never lets things drop.

The tomatoes are a bit watery and the toast is sodden. I am not sure whether to mention it.

The tomatoes are a bit watery and the toast is sodden – I say.

I hear the sound of grinding teeth.

And, I still can't seem to find the right simile. Haven't you any ideas?

He thinks for a moment. 'How about, "the knife pierced her skin"? Forget the simile. Make the verb do the work.'

And it did.

Nicki

A thin layer of sweat coats her upper lip as she walks out from the tube station and into the frozen evening air. It's one of the things she dislikes most about herself – the soft seeping liquid that pools, like clockwork, in the concave arch of her lower back, her shoulder blades, the space between her mouth and nostrils. It clogs her makeup and makes it pearl around her mouth in orangey clumps. Nothing she can do about it, obviously, but it's still embarrassing. Sweaty people are difficult to trust.

She doesn't know this part of the city well, and it's even more difficult to navigate in the dark. The station spills out onto a residential road with its grainy, white-washed houses, illuminated only by living-room lamps and the flicker of TVs. She makes her way too fast, unsurely. Checking her phone, turning it this way and that – is the arrow pointing in front of her or behind? – but never slowing down, not for a moment. Slowing down in the city means mugging, rape, or small talk with faces she only vaguely recognises.

As the hill steepens on her way from the station, the houses change, grainy white-wash replaced by exposed brickwork, superior (for some reason) because you can see the layers of cement, like a cadaver split open on the operating table. It's a top-floor flat. She dithers between the two bells – the scrawled labels have been eroded as to be illegible. She presses the top one, too hard, finger nail bending on the hard brass.

The silence that greets her is a hesitation, an utterly middle-class, who-is-calling-at-this-time-on-a-school-night sort of silence. And then, a woman's voice, high pitched, authoritative.

'Hello?'

'Hi, is that Nicki?'

'Yes, who's that?'

'My name's Emma. I'm, ah, a friend of Marie's.'

A different kind of silence this time. Thicker. A silence thick with thoughts, a silence that drags on.

'A friend of Marie's?'

'Yeah. I – I came to give you something. Of hers.'

'Of Marie's?'

The soft static of the telecom and the echo of breathing. The sweat seeps down her back with newly malicious vigour. God, how embarrassing if she isn't let in. Perhaps the woman can already tell the weakness, the hesitation in her voice, she will know that it is not even worth her time to –

'I'll buzz you in.'

Cold, cream-coloured hall. Post on the floor. Carpeted stairs that smell of damp. Light streaming from the upstairs door. Her head is spinning. She can only collate splintered impressions of things because there is a sense of something enormous all around her, pressing into the very pores of her flesh. A woman framed in the doorway as she draws level, shorter than expected, sandy corkscrew hair fading to grey. Round glasses that give a blinking, owlish look. Makeup-less face. Red cardigan, cable knit, bobbling. She feels self-conscious in her carefully chosen ensemble, the long coat, the scarf that matches the earrings. Too much, of course, for a random Tuesday evening, when it's obvious she hasn't come from work.

'Emma?'

'Yes. Hello. Nicki?' Her smile is forced, bending the corners of her mouth at dangerous angles. 'I'm sorry to barge in on you like this. I'm, ah, I'm actually Marie's daughter. Sorry. I should have said that on the –' *God.* 'I wonder if I could come in for a minute.'

The owlish eyes blink at her, assessing. Watery smile. The woman motions inwards, into the warmth beyond the door. 'Please.'

The flat is small and loudly decorated, red vases with

branches of pussy willow on the verge of death, mismatched crockery displayed smugly on the kitchen shelves, administrative looking papers spilling out across the table. The trappings of a home. She hovers in the doorway, eyes darting uncomfortably, and the woman notices.

'Won't you sit down? Would you like a drink? Tea or…something?'

'Just some water would be great. Thanks.' The forced smile still hovers on her mouth like the empty shell of something.

'I was sorry to hear about your mother.' The woman speaks without turning around, for which she is grateful because, of course, there are already tears in her eyes at the word *mother,* some weird primitive reaction that she can't yet shake. 'I saw it on the club Facebook page. She was a lovely woman. We hadn't spoken for a long time, I'm afraid, but we used to be… great friends.' She moves across the kitchen, face impassive, mismatching her words.

She was a lovely woman – one of many banal epithets that have echoed around her since her mother's death. People always erring on the side of caution. In death, her mother becomes nice, lovely, a very *kind* person. Her mother, voice reverberating with anger as she screamed about something, making the whole house shake. Her mother, spilling her barbed judgements on everything, all the time, getting her scorn over stuff like a red wine stain. Her mother, wiping sweat from her upper lip as she ran; curled up in depressed silence on the settee; flirting with other people's husbands. Her mother in church, tracing the rosary beads like a lover's features, mouth working fervently as she muttered the old familiar prayers. Her insane, difficult, beautiful mother, now compressed into *nice* and *lovely* and *condolences.*

Marie will be remembered as a dedicated runner and an even more dedicated friend. That's what it had said on the club Facebook page, written by one of her mother's old cronies. They had turned up at the funeral like a murder of crows, some of them still lean as whippets, some of them weak-kneed and running to fat after all these years. And in between the saccharine condolences, which passed over her almost unnoticed, she heard the gossip:

So strange that Nicki isn't here. Not when Marie loved her so much–

When Marie was so in love with her.

In. Love. The unmistakable emphasis on those two words have ripped the seams of her world open and sent its stuffing spilling out.

Her mother. With her endless fights and dates and discontent with men. She and her mother in their big, blow up arguments about feminism, each taking on the spitting insults of their generation. The two of them at Greenham Common, she tiny, a pit-stop on their way to see family in Oxford. The dark drabness of the business park. Her mother's voice shining as she described the peace camp, the women with their rainbow hair, the smell of wood smoke. The yellowed old scraps of newspaper that she had exhumed in a furious dig through her mother's study, the local rag with a black and white photo of a younger, thinner Marie and a younger, less grey-haired version of the woman in whose kitchen she sat, whose Facebook she had stalked and address she had tracked. SEX AND DRUGS IN THE PEACE CAMP. The glint in their eyes as they looked at each other, preserved like a corpse on the tattered page after forty years.

Other fragments. Sentences caught from books and her old lecture notes. *In many conscious raising groups, lesbianism was seen as the only solution to patriarchal oppression.* Saoirse had given her those books, back in the days, when they used to loll around on her flowery duvet covers, smoking out of her window and arguing congenially about the gender pay gap. They were at that stage of extreme youth where they seemed to be constantly morphing, their pale bodies just putty to be moulded into the fixed contours of adults. Saoirse had become a beautiful, spindly creature, her once childish face marked with an almost masculine beauty; and she herself, into what still felt like a parody of adulthood, a perfumed, jewellery-clad shadow.

Sometimes a picture of her old friend would pop up on her phone – raising her thin arms in ecstasy at a rave, or of her lovely features contorted into rage at a protest – and she would like it, bitterly, passively, before pushing it out of her mind.

They had not talked for years. Hardly at all since that day in her room, slightly high and dancing around hysterically to a Joni Mitchell record, when Saoirse had kissed her, with her bony body half covering hers on the bed and her arms digging into the mattress. And the overwhelming pressure that filled her stomach as they had kissed, the new awareness of her mouth, the nerve endings that seemed to be pushing out of her skin. The feeling that their bodies might actually seep into each other, molecule by molecule, and that it might not be such a bad thing.

And always her mother, even then. Her mother's mouth moving over the prayers. Their arguments, phrases like *intersectional* and *women's spaces* and *biological man*. The dream-like image of her mother meeting Saoirse, eyes widening in imaginary horror, mouth twisting cruelly. That same mouth beaming when she brought Sam home for the first time. Sam, who was tall and solid and decidedly unbeautiful, and who walked her home from parties and always wore a condom and didn't need to be convinced to meet her family actually, because he genuinely wanted to. Who had captured her mother's heart because he was *reliable* and *dependable* and all the other words with *-able* suffixes that were so unlike her mother's grubby romantic past. Who stood obliviously with his arm around her as their friends made homophobic jokes in the kitchen. Who she married, in part, to see her mother beaming with pride when she glanced back from the altar, tears glimmering in eyes obscured by a stupid teal hat bought especially for the day. Who no longer, if he ever had, made her nerve endings push out of her skin when he kissed her – if anything, kissing him fixed them more solidly in place, reinforcing the structure of her body, pushing it back into its confines.

Always, always her mother and her secrets. Her mother and her lies.

'Thanks,' she says. 'That's very kind of you.' Because there is nothing else to say, she realises, in a sudden rush of relief. Because her mother is dead – because she herself is married, which in itself is another kind of death – because nothing can be said to the woman before her that will change those facts. And there is beauty in the sense of finality that washes over her, the absolute relinquishment of something hard in her chest.

'Very kind of you,' she says again. Because that is all she can say.

Love in Paris

Sam Maxwell patted the little box in his pocket for the third time in a minute. Its presence was both reassuring and terrifying. Two thousand nine hundred and ninety-five euros. Five thousand bucks, give or take. The jewellers, which had caught his eye as he walked from Paris's Saint-Germain-des-Prés metro station, was called Bijou Daphne. The woman inside, Marie, had showed him the ring, vintage Art Deco she said, with a row of tiny diamonds set into a gold band. One wave of plastic and it was his.

Shops like that were usually invisible to Sam. But this one had a wood façade, the colour of burgundy grapes. The sun had dazzled the portico invitingly. It was like an invisible force had guided him in. Sam patted his precious cargo again, just to check it was still there.

He hadn't planned on buying Claire a ring today. This sort of behaviour wasn't like Sam at all. He'd never bought jewellery, for anyone, ever. Least of all an engagement ring. Did it have to be an engagement ring? Perhaps he could just give it to her as a gift. Casually. Just casually give the woman you love a five-thousand-dollar diamond ring. Nothing strange about that. If you were James Bond.

Sam crossed the road, passing a woman in long gloves, pulling a dog. In an empty brasserie, waiters were laying tables for lunch. The streets here were narrow, so that the yellow sun couldn't quite claw all the way down the prim stone façades of the Haussmannian apartments.

It bothered Sam that they were spending the second day of their vacation apart. Things had started badly. Claire kept on about the thinness of the towels in the hotel. She wouldn't leave it alone. So they agreed to do their own thing for the morning.

She'd explore the Galleries Lafayette, take some photos, and he would go and see Notre Dame, or whatever was left to look at since the fire.

Sam had a thing for old buildings that Claire didn't share. They didn't have a whole lot of interests in common. This wasn't the issue, though. Nor was it her disappointment in the Grand Hotel des Balcons. Grand, it turned out, in name alone. Fundamentally, Sam was predictable. He didn't try often enough to surprise her. And when he did try, even his efforts were predictable. Like this trip. She'd guessed it first time when he had sprung it on her.

He patted the little box again. She wouldn't see this coming in a million years. Partly because they'd rarely talked about marriage, beyond agreeing it wasn't important. But mostly because such acts of largesse were entirely out of character for Sam. Maybe this was what romance was. Pure romance, not the Valentine's Day kind. An act so spontaneous neither side could have predicted it. Sam had strolled into Bijou Daphne on a whim. Even he couldn't pinpoint why. He pictured the look of genuine shock, disbelief even, on Claire's face, when he gave her the ring. A look that melted into delight. A look that said, "I thought I knew you, but I was wrong".

Sam turned on to narrow Rue de Buci, which, according to the map on his phone, would take him most of the way to the Seine. A woman, about Claire's age, came out of an expensive-looking boutique and lit a cigarette. The scene had a cinematic quality, which Sam, as unseen observer, revelled in. He wondered about the woman's life, where she was going next and who she would meet. That's someone to whom you could give a diamond ring, causally, over dinner. Tell her she looked lovely. Just a little something to set off that dress. Stop. He was being predictable again.

Sam wondered how he would give the ring to Claire. Maybe just leave it on the pillow. Absent-mindedly. No, not the hotel. At dinner then. Ideally, it would be a quiet little place, chef-owner. Local crowd. Tables simply laid. Nothing fussy. A candle. Good bread. Wine. He didn't actually know anywhere like this. And they'd need a vegetarian option for Claire. He'd have to check online. It was Friday, too, he realised. Booking somewhere at short notice would be a challenge. And he didn't speak French.

Up ahead Sam saw passing traffic, and, beyond, that a glint of river. A Société Générale bank had an advert for a credit card in the window. Sam felt a squeeze of doubt. Five thousand dollars. A fifth of everything he had saved. Had he made a terrible mistake? He thought back to Bijou Daphne, the way Marie's fingers held the ring. Her soft voice and broken English. Already it had assumed a dreamlike quality in his mind. No. This was meant to be. This was important. Defining, even. This was happening.

Sam strode through a gap in traffic and onto the Pont Saint-Michel, the short bridge that joined Paris's left bank to the Île de la Cité. Looking east, he saw the twin spires of Notre Dame for the first time. They looked fine. Normal. Any damage wasn't visible from here. He touched the box in his pocket. There were more tourists here than on Rue de Buci. The sight of them jarred Sam. He looked down at his own sandals, his khaki shorts, and made a mental note to dress better, from now on.

Across the bridge, Sam took the Quai de Marche Neuf, Notre Dame rising up in front of him as he walked. A tourist rickshaw slowed down alongside, ringing its bell. Sam met the driver's eye then looked away. Words were muttered before it pedalled off. He felt for the box again. Maybe there wasn't any real rush. He could take the ring back home with him. Wait for the right time. He played this out in his mind. Giving the ring to Claire in a few days or weeks, she'd ask why. Why did you wait? What could he say? The time was now. Paris. The sunlight in the trees, Bijou Daphne, the lady with the cigarette. And Sam, unpredictable, unknowable. He was riding a wave of inspiration that would have to break before long. And the key to it all was contained within this little box.

On the cobbled plaza overlooked by Notre Dame, Sam stopped and stood for a while, letting the crowds eddy and whirl around him. All these people and their stories. He relaxed. He liked to be surrounded by strangers. It made him feel more at ease with himself. The problem with Claire, well, with anyone you share all those everyday moments with, is that if you aren't careful, your edges get soft. Something important can ebb away, little by little, with each passing day. The ring would fix that.

Would it though? However he did it - down on one knee, hide the ring inside a soufflé - what reaction could he reasonably expect? A proposal in Paris! He could see Claire's eyes roll. And the thing with a proposal, it's not just giving something, it's a transaction. Those little diamonds make their own demands. Never mind that they were born of a spirit more spontaneous, reckless even. A spirit that sparked in one particular moment in time, and took him into Bijou Daphne.

Sam circled around the north side of the cathedral, away from the crowds. Here was where the worst of the damage revealed itself. It was quiet. Sad, even. He felt like he was intruding into another person's grief. Sam kept walking and put another bridge between him and the broken cathedral, drawn towards the convivial red awnings with gold trim of La Brasserie de l'Isle Saint-Louis. Waiters in black waistcoats and white aprons tended tables, squeezed close together, under a horse chestnut tree. It was on the corner, a perfect cliché of a place that he took a table by the road. Sitting down was a relief. A waiter came over smartly. The lilt of conversations, Sam couldn't understand, were joined by the strains of an accordion. Over by the river, a man in a beret played for passing tourists. It was corny but so what.

Sam could return the ring to Bijou Daphne. Retrace his steps after he finishes his beer. A 35-minute walk, more or less. Forget this whole business, pretend it never happened. Marie would understand. Everyone has second thoughts. He imagined going back there, seeing that the sunlight had moved, and the sparkle was gone. He sipped his beer. Here he was, he thought, by himself, at La Brasserie de l'Isle Saint-Louis. For once he wasn't sure where he was heading, only that he knew it wasn't backwards.

He could always just hang on to the ring, a quirky memento. Put it somewhere safe, sell it later, make a loss, of course. He watched a woman arrive, greeting a man at a table nearby. They kissed, both cheeks. Her smile was open and wholehearted. He was in a work suit, she more casual. The sun hit the big tree above them just perfectly now. Claire would like this place, he thought. The polite waiters, the tree, the possibilities. Sam felt the urge to message her. Only he'd have to ask for the wi-fi code. She had suggested at the airport that they buy SIM cards, but he'd told her they always rip you off.

Sam swallowed the last of his beer. He wished he had a cigarette, though he hadn't smoked for years. He put a ten-euro note under the ashtray and left the brasserie without turning back. He walked towards the riverbank. Something had compelled him all the way here, like the waters of the Seine. He took the box out of his pocket, opened it, and looked at the ring for the first time since he'd bought it. It was more ordinary now. Just a little something. He turned it over in his hand.

Leaning on the stone wall beside the river, Sam flicked the ring up in the air. It caught the light. He held his breath. It came down, down, and landed back in his hand. He turned away and walked in the direction of his hotel. The man, playing the accordion, met his eyes as he went past. Sam dropped the ring into the case, earning a smile in return, the kind of smile you'd get if it was a one-euro piece, and the music kept playing.

It Would Take a Miracle

Dotty walked briskly through the tall fretwork cemetery gates, the traffic lulling behind her. She shifted the shopper, heavy wi bottled water and wet wipes, to her other arm. She couldnae rely on the tap here. When she was done she'd have a wee nosy at the new dug graves. After all, what was the point of those lovely flowers and cards if naebody read or enjoyed them? The deid person was past that, the kin were away home, leaving only locals and angels - or devils - depending on where you ended up. She looked to the heavens; no often she got a dry day to linger and pay respects even if it was cold and grey, the sky heavy wi gloom.

Anyway, she was glad to be out the house as her heart was roasted wi aw they forms. Annoying that the Department of Work and Pensions had to send them, couldnae pick them up at the Post Office. They said to phone in your application, but she was nae guid on the phone, couldnae follow what was being said and aye mucked it up. But twenty-eight pages?

She might no bother applying at aw.

Just starve to death, be found skin and bone on the kitchen floor.

Doctor James was a lovely man, insisted she apply, even though she tellt him she wouldnae get anything. 'I'm no sick. It's aw in the heid, son,' she said. 'I can walk, cook and clean, so I can still work, don't need nae Personal Independence Payments.'

Och, they were poor souls here, a few new ones the day, nae heidstones yet, easy to spot wi their carpet of flowers. The bright colours drew her eye past the drab stones, the dirt, the grass. She smiled, it was guid to spit in the eye of death.

The silence was pierced by the shrill cries of gulls overhead and the lament of a dove. No a soul around. The grave-diggers were usually about, having a fag, leaning on their spades. No a job Dotty'd like, though it depended on how you looked at it. You could take the view you were digging graves or, take the other view, you were a gardener planting, cutting grass, or landscaping. No digging in the daytime, mind. They did that early morning, then covered the open grave wi a bright green tarpaulin. She might just get cremated and save a lot of carry-on.

She gathered herself and ambled around the corner to her mam and da's grave where she dropped her bag, leant doon and took out a bunch of droopy red peonies, the water bottle and her antiseptic wet wipes. After a wee clean-up of the stone and a change of the water in the vase it was aw hunky-dory. Except the lettering looked dull. She knelt in front of the stone wi a pot of Brasso and a cloth and rubbed the letters until they shone.

Thank God for wet wipes and bottled water. And Brasso, of course.

She stood up straight. 'Mam, you were poor aw your days, but I don't remember you ever had to rely on the government or go to a food bank for your dinner. Last Monday I hung about so long in the rain I was fair soaked when I went in that door. There arenae the shifts at work. My wages clear ran out.' She made a slow sign of the cross. 'Bye Mam and Da. See you next time.'

Dotty stepped along the path, turned right, and zig zagged through some gravestones, 'Sorry, sorry,' until she spotted the line of Scots pine that sheltered Alec and the wean. 'Nae tears, Dotty. It's aw so long ago, but also no so long ago. A well-kept grave, wouldnae have it any other way.'

She cleaned the black panel, polished the lettering, picked off spots of damp, got up off her knees, gripping the curved edge of the gravestone, and brushed away dirt and grass from her slacks. Her heid bowed, she made the sign of the cross. 'See you next time, my darlings.'

Today she felt like lingering, so decided on a wee saunter in the auld lanes where rich folk were buried under big heidstones adorned wi angels and cherubs. Slowing to a stop, she peered at a grubby angel, years of green mould running down the legs and ower her cherubic face. Her wings were black wi it. Dotty supposed there was naebody left to clean it up. She moved in closer. Aye, a few of them in there. Woolfries, Mary-Anne, six months of age. Died in 1937. And a brother, Nicholas, died age seven months, and two more infants. Bless that poor mother, she was there too, 1945. And a father, 1960. Heartache came whether or no you were rich.

Hey, that was fair annoying the state of that angel. She could clean the wee face if she stood on that tree trunk. What did folk do in the auld days before wet wipes? Aye, her mother had auld rags in bleach constantly. Choking smell through the house aw day long. Probably where Dotty got her obsession, as Alec had called it. *Dotty stop cleaning, the place is like an operating theatre.*

'Order and cleanliness are what keeps us alive,' she'd replied.

What was that there? Och, only a wee robin perched on the angel's heid. So tame, those birds. But this one had shat aw doon the angel's face. Bugger. 'Shoo, shoo.' It hopped away, miffed. 'Shoo, shoo…' He was flying away, no… landed ontae the next stone waiting for her to leave. She wasnae going nowhere. That would definitely need cleaned up now.

Dotty stepped on the grass, climbed ontae the tree trunk, leant ower, rubbed the angel's face, and scrubbed again. The surface was warm under her fingers, no like stone at aw. And they flecks on the face wouldnae rub off, no matter how hard Dotty scrubbed. They couldnae be? Aye, freckles. That was awfy clever of the stonemason. The stone ringlets had a tone of red about them. Hardly, must've been the sun. But there wasnae any sun, just grey sky up there. Maybe a lamp was shining some place. The eyes were like sapphires, glass of course. Mind, that was unusual on a statue.

It had lashes, fair and silken. Brushed the back of Dotty's

hand like a whisper. She drew it back fast.

Christ almighty, the statue was yawning. Dotty cried out, 'Get doon, quick. Oh my, I must be hallucinating. It's they tablets.' She backed away, stepped off the trunk, and tottered to the bench to rest a minute, her eyes closed.

Phew, she was away wi the fairies. The doc was right. There, the angel was back to what she was. A statue. Dotty's heart's drummed, the form business had been too much. Two or three shifts would do her, there was aye the food bank if she got stuck again.

She took a peek; it was just a statue.

A loud bang, what the Hell?

Gravestones shook, Tarmacadam cracked, a deep rumble ran underfoot.

The angel shivered, fluttered, her wings quivered, unfolded but strained as if stuck. She flexed arms and shoulders and stretched her neck. A squeak, a rattle, crumbling cement, a crack on the plate, dust flying, and the heidstone split in half. Now, a sharp snap like breaking bone; the feet were loose from the plate, the wings spreading and…

Dotty screamed, 'Doon, Dotty doon. Watch your heid. She's up, she's away.'

Blinking uncontrollably, Dotty lay on her side on the bench. 'There, there. No, still gone. The angel's gone.'

Only crumbling cement, cracks, and choking dust remained.

Dotty sat up, coughed, spat, fumbled in her bag for baby wipes and wiped dirt from her face.

The rumbling underfoot had stopped. She tried to get up on her feet but her legs were water. 'Maybe God didnae like me walking on the graves. Sorry, sorry, in the name of the Father, the Son, the Holy Ghost…' Where was everyone? How come no one had heard the noise? The place was still deserted, though Dotty's vision was clouded, and she couldnae see more than a few yards around her.

Out of the fog of dust came a friendly voice. 'Hello.'

Dotty turned from side to side. 'Oh hello, I'm so glad to see a living soul. Mother of God…' It was her off the plinth. Dotty's heart raced but paralysis stayed her joints, and it was a long way to the safety of the main road.

The angel perched down beside her on the bench. Dotty slid away as far as she could; the wings took up a lot of space, and Dotty wasnae for soiling that delicate stuff.

She was put in mind of sitting on a bus beside a drunk, trying to pretend you werenae there, ignoring the fact the drunk was stinking. Though this angel smelt like freesia petals. Dotty glanced ower, och no, the wee soul was greetin.

Dotty fished in her pocket and held out the pack of baby wipes. The angel reached for it wi graceful fingers, and extracted one, two, three. Dotty tore off the last one for her. How pretty the wee thing was, pale and slender. But that might've been an illusion as she was hovering now in front of the bench, feet off the ground, wings fluttering either side: feathery blues, pinks, and greens displacing what remained of the settling smog. The angel dried her eyes and handed Dotty the wipes. Stuffing them in her bag, Dotty leant hard against the bench. The cemetery was deathly quiet, no sign of the robin, no dove calls, no even any seagulls or ravens.

Just Dotty and an angel, an angel woken wi a wet wipe. Dotty wondered what she could've done wi a bottle of Domestos. 'How did you manage to get off that pedestal, hen?'

'You freed me.'

'Me?'

'Yes, you showed me a kindness.' She perched on the arm of the bench, wings at rest.

'So, like rubbing a lamp. Are you a genie?'

She giggled, tears forgotten. 'Not at all, I'm an angel. Seraphim, to be exact.'

Dotty remembered something about seraphims from her catechism; they were pals wi cherubims. Guid angels. 'Very nice.'

This was a wee bit embarrassing. The angel probably wasnae there and Dotty'd be caught talking to hersel. The doc was right and she should apply for that PIP benefit. If she put this hallucination on the form, she'd qualify no bother. She closed her eyes, and blinked them open slowly. The angel was still there. If she wasnae real, Dotty'd best get on, ignore the vision. If she was real, then she'd best get on. Dragging hersel up, she said, 'Nice to meet you, I'll be on my way now.'

Walking towards the gates, Dotty didnae look back, but wing vibration stirred the air behind her, from one side to the other. The angel swung out in front of Dotty's face and hovered, stopping her in her tracks. Dipping her heid the seraphim said, 'Thank you, Dotty,' and disappeared.

Dotty's heart sank, jumped, sank again. She'd better go home before she collapsed or saw devils. Just as she exited the big gates there was a commotion. Three cemetery workers bashed out of their yard, one on his phone. 'There's been an explosion. Fire brigade, aye. A grave's blown up, aye aye…'

Dotty put a step on it.

When she reached her house, she clinked the gate and walked up the path, unlocked the front door and let hersel in. A nasty shock greeted her in the lobby mirror. Her face and shoulders were caked in white dust and blood streaked her foreheid. She fingered her hairline: a cut nipped, but it had stopped bleeding.

She stepped on some envelopes, leant doon, and picked them up. One looked official. Inside was a letter. *Mrs Reid, you have been awarded the high rate of Personal Independent Payment, payable into your bank account from…*

She let it flutter to the table.

Unshackled

The New Woman

'Please.'

The word, spoken on a sob of desperation, went ignored. The woman scrambled from person to person, grabbing at hands, legs, feet.

'Help me…' she cried, grabbing Anokhi's ankle. 'Please.'

Anokhi didn't even blink. Her expression was tired, almost bored.

Then one of the men came forward and hauled the woman away. Her screams grew fainter. The sound of a sharp slap split the air. Everything went silent.

The five women standing around the chamber slowly returned to their rooms. The sun was setting – it was time to get to work.

Anokhi

When Anokhi brought her food hours later, the woman was huddled on the floor in a corner. Anokhi left the door open. The woman wouldn't try to run anymore. Anokhi placed the plate before the woman. She responded by curling tighter into herself.

'If you don't eat, you'll only feel worse,' Anokhi said, her voice soft.

'How can you do this?' The woman's eyes flashed with accusation. 'Why won't you help me?'

'Who sent you here?' Anokhi asked in response as she sat cross-legged, facing her.

The woman blinked. 'I…'

Anokhi nodded. She knew the pain of having to accept the words as reality, once spoken. 'A fake job offer abroad,' she said, reading the woman's face. 'Or some relative. An uncle. A cousin. A husband who sells you off after he's done with you on the wedding night.' The woman's breath caught.

Anokhi nodded again. 'For me,' she said, 'it was my father.'

'Your father?' the woman gasped.

'My mother named me Vidya. Knowledge.' Anokhi smiled without humour. 'She wanted me to study. My father wanted me to clean houses so that he had money for his gambling and drinking. One day, his gambling debt became too heavy. He beat my mother almost to death in anger. He beat me too. I woke up here. Anokhi glanced around the room. 'He got eighty-five thousand rupees for me. Ten thousand more than they'd promised because I was a virgin. He took the money, told me he'd kill my mother if I tried to return, and left. They named me Anokhi. Vidya died that day. No one helped me... that day or since.'

'So now *you* won't help anyone?' Disgust laced the woman's words.

'I *can't* help you,' Anokhi replied. 'No one can. You have to accept the truth – you now belong to Asha Madam and her goons. This is your life, Palak. That's your name now. They will *never* let you get away. You can accept that by yourself, or they'll make you accept it. *You* decide what happens to you. Eat your food, Palak,' she added softly. 'Asha Madam is waiting for you.'

Palak

Mumbai. The city that never sleeps was uncharacteristically quiet under a dark sky. Even the garish lights adorning the verandas and windows of the red-light district buildings were off.

Palak stepped across the threshold onto the roof terrace. Asha Madam was leaning against the waist-high wall at the far end, staring into the night. The man, who'd locked her in her room, stood against the adjacent wall. Palak could feel his eyes on her as she walked, Anokhi following her.

Asha Madam turned. 'Look at you,' she smiled. 'You look

much better now. Anokhi explained things to you?'

Palak nodded in silence.

'Good.s' Asha Madam spoke like she was talking to a child. 'She was just fourteen when she joined us, but she was so furious! She fought so hard to get away. My men didn't like it.' She laughed. 'Almost killed her a couple of times. But I stopped them. She is too beautiful! She eventually learned.' Asha Madam came to stand by Anokhi. 'And she's been such a good girl since.'

Anokhi dropped her gaze to her feet. In the moment before, Palak saw, in her eyes, why she'd been unable to help her, why she would *never* be able to help herself. She was terrified of these people.

And the last shred of doubt in her heart dissipated.

'Anokhi was right, Asha Madam,' Palak said. Anokhi looked up in question as Palak walked to the wall and turned to them. '*I* decide.'

Without another word, she fell back... over the wall and into the night.

Juhi

Palak's death was ruled an accident, the papers attested by a cop who got both money and free use of the women. Anokhi's life went on. She entertained and satisfied her clients, earning money for Asha and the men who kept them in line.

She smiled, she danced, she laughed... but something inside her had died with Palak.

She'd once convinced herself that whatever she did, she did to survive. But now, that survival seemed... pointless. Yet the terror she felt for the people who owned her wouldn't let her consider escape.

Anokhi was lost in the same internal battle that had plagued her for the past three months when a girl was shoved into her room. She jumped to her feet, staring from the girl sprawled across the floor to the man at her door.

'Clean this one up,' Jaggi roared. 'Talk some sense into her.

And not like you did with that other one! Little bitch bit me. Calm her down before I kill her!'

Anokhi stared at the quivering, crying mess. The girl looked barely twelve. She pushed herself up on shaking arms and crawled across the floor.

'Help me,' she sobbed, grabbing Anokhi's feet. 'Please.'

Anokhi froze, an image of Palak's tear-stained face coming back to her. Then, she grabbed the girl by her arms and half-lifted her, sitting her at the edge of the bed.

'What's your name?' she asked, the futile question spoken before she could stop herself.

'Juhi,' the girl replied, wiping tears from her face.

'Who brought you here?'

'My uncle,' Juhi replied, her voice hoarse from crying. 'He moved here from the village many years ago. He said he will help me get into a good city school. The school in my village is not very good. My mother wants me to study. But when we got off the train…' Juhi broke down into sobs and fell against Anokhi, desperately holding onto her. Anokhi draped her arms around the girl, her heart beating rapidly. For five years she'd watched silently as woman after woman was betrayed, and she had turned away from all of them… just like those who had brought them to this hell. All because she couldn't overcome the fear of how they'd tortured her until they'd broken the spirit, the spirit her mother had nurtured in her against all odds. In that moment, she realised that Palak had ended her life in one, quick moment. Anokhi was dying every day, under her own terror and the inhumanity.

When Juhi finally stopped crying, she pulled back to look at Anokhi. 'What's your name, *Didi*?'

The nineteen-year-old girl who had lost her childhood too soon stared into the eyes of her past self.

'Vidya,' she smiled, the agony buried within her disappearing. 'My name is Vidya.'

Saket

Saket had been an independent investigative journalist for four years. An intrepid reporter, he chose to immerse himself in the murkiest parts of society to find justice for the voiceless. With his team, he'd helped the police close twenty-five cases. Some cops thought him a partner, some, a nuisance.

When his phone rang at some late hour, he picked up instantly, assuming the unknown number to be an anonymous tip or informant. He hadn't heard the voice in four years that said his name. But he recognised it immediately. He'd posed as a client every other night for two weeks, trying to get her to talk, to give him the names which would expose the whole brothel and trafficking ring. But she'd never given them up. Until now.

'Anokhi?'

'Help me get her out,' she said hurriedly. 'Wednesday morning. At four. Come to the back entrance and wait. I *will* come. Please, take her somewhere safe. Not to the cops here.'

'Who is she?' Saket asked, his stomach twisting in concern.

'She's *twelve*, Saket. Just twelve.'

Pain washed over him. 'I'll be there.'

'Saket,' Anokhi took a deep breath, 'she'll have the list with her. All the information you wanted. Send them all to Hell!'

The line went dead.

Vidya

A few drinks were all it took to make Jaggi drop his guard and break Asha Madam's rule – don't use the merchandise. Once he fell asleep, Vidya silently slipped off the bed, got dressed, and grabbed the keys from his pants' pocket. She crept back to her own room.

Moments later, looking around like a deer wary of a predator, she quietly led Juhi through the dark house. The back door led to a long, narrow alley filled with garbage bags. It was locked from the inside, its only key gripped in Vidya's trembling hand. Throwing one last look over her shoulder, she quickly opened the padlock. It clanged loudly, and Vidya knew her countdown had begun. She forced the rusty bolt open, ignoring its expected screeching sound.

Throwing the door open, she stepped out, Juhi in tow. Her eyes searched desperately in the darkness. And then something moved. A man stepped into the soft moonlight. His features became clearer with every step, and relief flooded over Vidya.

Juhi had skulked behind the older woman, untrusting of the stranger. Vidya turned, falling to her haunches to look into her eyes.

'It's okay,' she said, forcing the fear out of her voice. 'You'll be safe with him, I promise.'

Juhi looked at Saket. Then turning to Vidya, she nodded.

'Keep her safe, please.' Vidya gently placed Juhi's hand in Saket's outstretched one.

Saket could only nod as he looked at the young girl he'd known, now a grown woman.

Something had been broken within her. But not anymore.

'You?' he finally managed to ask.

Vidya's smile disclosed her acceptance as tears sprang to her eyes. A loud thud sounded before she could respond.

'Go!' she hissed. 'Now!'

Saket turned and rushed down the alley, as fast as Juhi's small legs could go. Vidya's gaze followed them.

'Whore!'

She whirled around to face Jaggi, his face red with anger.

'Please,' Vidya begged, folding her hands. 'She's just a little girl.'

'Get out of the way!'

His slap made her skin burn with pain. Her head hit the door frame and she fell to her side.

'Vidya *Didi*!' Juhi broke away from Saket, crying. She ran a few steps before Saket grabbed her. He saw the large man in the distance. Vidya's words filled his head. *Keep her safe, please.* Saket lifted the girl into his arms, turned, and ran.

Vidya lashed out, desperate, as Jaggi leaped over her. She

grabbed his ankle and was dragged a couple of feet across the rough ground before she pulled with all her strength, bringing Jaggi to his knees. Forcing herself to her feet, she stumbled forward to stand between him and Juhi.

'No, Jaggi,' she said, her eyes like fire. 'I won't let you get to her.'

Jaggi jumped to his feet and raised a gun to her chest.

'Move,' he spat.

Vidya glanced over her shoulder. Saket and Juhi were almost at the end of the alley. A minute more and Jaggi would never get to them. She turned to look at the gun pointed at her and knew what she had to do.

'No.'

She took a step forward, gripped his hands to hers - and pulled the trigger. The shot cracked through the quiet night. Still gripping the gun, Vidya pulled Jaggi with her as she fell back. His free hand stopped his fall, but he struggled to pull the gun from her grip.

Vidya twisted to look out at the alleyway. She saw Saket turn to look at her, shielding Juhi's gaze from the sight. Then, they disappeared into the night.

Vidya smiled with happiness, happiness she hadn't felt in five years. As she let go of the gun, only one thought came to her with her last breath.

I decide.

Faithful

New Year's Eve

Sometime before midnight, he walks out onto a balcony. He climbs onto the ledge and stands there – on the tails of an old year, inching precariously toward the new. He spots me below, on the other side of the street. He stops. It has been raining all night. The road holds reflections of the city skyline on the ground, like a dazzling kaleidoscopic painting on a wet canvas. Water drips into the drains, reflecting lights like electric fire. He climbs off the ledge; his eyes remain fixed on me. He smiles, but looks embarrassed. Across the road from me, he is two floors up from a tree-lined boulevard. He disappears back into his apartment. I return my attention to the street again. Most of the snow has melted during the day, and now a glossy sheen covers the roads. A small group of revellers come into view, giggling and swigging drinks. They kick and throw what's left of the snow at one another. Later on it becomes busy. People are rushing hither-thither, I guess from one party to another, before the midnight hour strikes. He has returned to the balcony, now brandishing a flute of Champagne in his hand. As the clock strikes midnight, I hear cheering from the cafés and bars. He raises his glass to me and mouths, 'Happy New Year.' Somewhere fireworks go off. I watch their dazzling colours reflect in the apartment windows in front of me. I scan window to window, stealing delight from celebrations never intended for me. He remains out in the cold for another hour or so before waving goodbye and returning to his apartment.

Spring

Life has returned. People on the street look fresh and rested from their winter hibernation. It's as if they too are sprouting the first shoots of optimism for what the year has in store.

One hazy morning, I am forced forward with a violent strike. I'm stripped – my clothes torn away with impatient hands. An overweight woman huffs and puffs as she picks up my scattered clothes from the floor. She leaves. I'm left naked. A few people in the street notice me, but no one cares. Later that morning, a young store assistant walks over to me. With gentle hands, she slips my arms into a white crepe shirt. The two top buttons left undone. She lowers me onto the worn carpet to get a pair of tights on me. This is something she hasn't got the knack of. It takes her a long while to get them on; she has to wiggle my feet about to get them over my heels. It gives me a chance to look around the store. The other models are poorly made, and some are downright grotesque – missing limbs and decapitated bodies. I try not to judge, but some of the clothes they wear – good heavens! None of their outfits match. Once I am back upright, she pulls a knee-length blue pencil skirt around my waist. The look is complete with a matching blazer. A business suit! I feel power and authority hum through my plastic body. The young woman repositions my arms before leaving. I now stand with authority, arms folded across my chest – the ruthless stance of the modern business age.

He says he wants to be my boyfriend. He tells me he loves me. Maybe he does. In the evenings I usually see him. He once told me this is his favourite moment of the day. I want to be a good girlfriend, so it is my favourite moment of the day also. When he first came into the store, he was nervous. It was only a couple of days into New Year. On a meandering journey towards my window, he stopped several times. He pretended to look at clothes on a rack or to look at his watch. When he stood by my side, he introduced himself, almost in a whisper. He often glanced around the store and touched his face when he spoke. He told me he felt the need to explain his actions from New Year's Eve. He said it had been six months since he last spoke to Maria, his ex-girlfriend; we don't like her or her new boyfriend, Kenny. He tells me they had been through difficult times and assumed they would get through this one. They had had a fantastic social life, both together and separately. Then one night, she left without warning. She phoned him two days later to explain that she'd met someone else. My boyfriend imagined Maria and her new boyfriend celebrating New Year's Eve together. Maybe on some exotic beach, drinking fluorescent cocktails and giggling under a warm sun. He said, that night in his apartment, he could hear their laughter echoing around his head. He said he would never have gone through with jumping. He tells me he is dependable.

Summer

The endless days and humid nights can mean only one thing: summer has finally arrived. It warms the street, igniting the weeds and grasses that grow in the cracked pavement.

Customers now fill the store daily. They rush about, caught up in the heat and frenzy of the long days. Gone is my business attire. The young assistant has given me a beautiful cotton dress and matching sandals. My legs feel the warmth of the morning sun, shining through the store window. I also have a new posture! It's the pose of someone who should be carefree and ready to embrace the world – a hand on my hips, one arm flying in the air and a twist in my waist. The dress and happy-go-lucky demeanour do have their downsides; the men on the street leer at my breasts and hips and partially exposed legs as they walk past the window. My boyfriend never leers. When he tells me he loves me, I can see happiness on his face. There is no reply. My lips do not move. My face remains static. None of this matters. For the first time, he visits me during the workday. He should be in the office, but he is ill. He suffers from hay fever and has taken two days off. He comments on my new dress; he likes my new look. My boyfriend has more confidence now. He no longer appears awkward. He stands up straight. One day he says, 'I got you this.' He puts a thin silver bracelet on my wrist and beams. When he leaves, I hear the women from the department store snigger. They call my boyfriend a 'weirdo' and an 'oddball'. He sometimes talks about all the little things Maria said that upset him. He has a long list. I think this is why I appeal to him. Outside, people's responses are unpredictable, frightening or demeaning in his world. Wrong reactions seem to upset my boyfriend. I give him a predictable comfort; I have never said an unkind word to him. I cannot offend him by being aloof or giving him an upsetting look. Our relationship is sterile, but clean, and free from the usual strains.

Autumn

The nights grow darker, with the last of the summer fruits eaten. Leaves lay glossy on the rain-washed street.

I have a seductive bedroom look, a sensual bodysuit with a strappy open front and a keyhole crisscross-lacing back. It's made to thrill, complete with a bold red robe. My hand has been placed across the top of my chest, with the other resting by my side. It is a beautiful pose to bring out my desirability and femininity.

My boyfriend is taken aback the first time he sees my new look. He is nervous, like the first time we met in the store. After a few more visits, he gains confidence. When no one in the store is looking, he tenderly strokes my leg. Sometimes he holds my hand as he tells me about his day. His palms are always sweaty. He is thoughtful. He always asks me questions like, 'Are you warm enough?' He never looks at others as he walks over. His passionate eyes are permanently fixed on mine. Does it matter if I'm not real? It doesn't matter to my boyfriend. When a man stares at a naked woman, is it her personality he is interested in? Is a woman's personality not something that some men wish to escape from? One time his phone rang while we were together. He pulled it out and scoffed at it. 'Now she calls when I'm finally happy again.' He hangs up and replaces the phone into his jacket. I heard today he might be going to

Hong Kong for a business trip next month. 'It's up in the air right now, but if it does happen, I'll bring you back something nice.' His gaze goes down my body before he looks back up at me and caresses my cheek. 'It'll only be for a week... Absolutely not, work only. I have no intention of visiting those places.'

Winter

The bitter wind outside reminds us that winter is approaching fast. I observe frost glistening on the pavement in the morning half-light. Within the apartment block across the road are every child's Christmas dreams.

A new store assistant dresses me. She is middle-aged and has a large face with plump lips and a thick mask of makeup. She handles me firmly but not with malice. She turns around as she removes my lingerie. I inspect the other models – they've not had a good year. Most have cracks on their skin, and all have scraggly hair. When the assistant is finished, I am back, staring out the window. I'm wearing a beautiful vintage-inspired mint-green winter coat, a perfect antidote to any winter blues. Made from luxurious, soft materials with a detachable hood and faux-fur trim, she has even teamed my outfit with a pair of matching gloves and a cosy knitted scarf.

Snow begins to fall. I watch as cascading flakes dance on the wind. My boyfriend is walking down the street, plumes of his breath rise into the slate-grey sky. I see him approaching behind me in the reflection of the store window. We look like a washed-out photograph. When he does turn to face me, he still has snowflakes in his hair. He tells me he likes my new coat and says I look *homely*. Then he explains that he turned down his business trip because he couldn't be away from me. The way my boyfriend looks, tells me I should be happy, so I am happy. He reminds me it's been almost a year since we first met. He tells me he has a particular question to ask me tomorrow. My boyfriend looks excited.

When the store is closed at night, a middle-aged store assistant talks to some men; I hear them say I will be relocated to a new flagship store in a big city. I take a last look across at my boyfriend's apartment. I guess I am also capable of betrayal. I wonder what he wanted to ask me tomorrow. I'm escorted to a van.

As I am driven away into the winter night, I guess we'll see how much he really does love me, as he said he does.

The Misbegotten

They called her Pajarita. Little bird. Her mother hadn't expected her to survive, so small was she at birth. And yet she had grown to be an inquisitive young girl with an infectious laugh and the sweetest of voices that echoed through the house like the chatter of a songbird in spring.

Maria Romero, the old woman who lived at the foot of the hill, told anyone who would listen that the child was cursed because she had been conceived out of wedlock. She would, said Maria Romero, bring nothing but trouble: *la pequeña bastarda.*

So when Pajarita fell from the first floor window of the house next door, the wooden shutters open wide before being closed against the blistering afternoon sun, Maria Romero added a dash of aguardiente to her coffee and thanked the Lord for taking mercy on the village.

Pajarita - the little bastard - had been playing with her friend when she had tumbled from the opening, falling the height of two grown men, and hitting her head on the small metal table below at which Senor Rodriguez, the man of the house, had been drinking with his old friend, Sanchez.

It took a moment for Senor Rodriguez, and several moments more for Sanchez, to realise the gravity of the situation. They were drunk, as usual, having taken their crops to the market in Manizales at six o'clock that morning and fetched a good price from the stallholder. But now, like a hatchling thrown from its nest by a cuckoo, there lay on the dusty ground before them, a motionless child, small and pinkish-blue. It had happened so suddenly and so noiselessly - apart from the sickening crack of the little girl's skull on the edge of the table - they could not at first make sense of the scene. Then Senor Rodriguez flew from his rickety wooden chair and scooped the poor child from the ground, cradling her in his arms.

His wife - Isabela - and his daughter, who just moments before had been playing catch with Pajarita in the front room upstairs, emerged from the open door, with hands over their mouths, as if to prevent the horror from entering their souls.

'Go for the doctor,' Isabela instructed her daughter. 'Fetch the priest,' she told Sanchez. 'Give her to me,' she said to her husband, 'and go find her mother.'

Pajarita's mother, Gabriela Aguilar, was a cleaner for the old man who lived in the big stone house on the hill above the village. Rumour had it that he had been a recluse since his wife died in childbirth twenty years earlier. Maria Romero told anyone who would listen that the old man worshipped the Devil and roamed the hills naked at night, howling to the moon like a wounded dog.

But when Senor Rodriguez got to the house, there was no sign of Gabriela Aguilar, nor anyone else. So he ran to the small cottage that nestled in the field below where he believed the old man's nephew, Nestor, lived - hoping that he at least would know where Gabriela Aguilar might be - which was when he saw her kissing the nephew goodbye.

Embarrassed, he waited until she'd reached the road before he called to her. 'Gabriela,' he said. 'You must come quickly. Pajarita has had a fall.' And the two of them started downhill, Gabriela running faster than Senor Rodriguez, of course, which spared them both the difficulty of explaining what had happened: how Pajarita had been injured in the care of the Rodriguez family who minded the child while Gabriela was out working; and how Gabriela had come to be with Nestor, when she should have been cleaning the old man's house.

By the time they reached the village, the priest had already arrived and was administering the last rites on the assumption that the little girl would surely die, when the radical young doctor appeared and pushed him aside, bringing the child back to life, at least to the point of getting her to breathe again. Maria Romero later claimed that the godless doctor, who was known to treat the rebels in the hills, had dragged Pajarita from beyond the gates of Hell, where the *pequeña bastarda* was destined to reside without the church, and that this was the source of the curse that subsequently befell the village.

Pajarita remained in bed for a month after the accident, speechless but for the occasional groan in the dead of night. Her mother, Garbriela Aguilar, slept on the floor beside her, hoping - and praying - that she might somehow recover, but in her heart, she knew that Pajarita's spirit had left her fragile body, as a fledgling leaves an empty nest. Maria Romero had it that the soul of the *pequeña bastarda* took the form of an owl after dark, roaming the village in search of fresh prey, and neighbours, who had seen the owl, or knew of those that had, took to locking their pets indoors at night.

Suspicion and distrust amongst the villagers grew like cancer. Gabriela Aguilar, distressed at the fate of her little girl, blamed Isabela for failing to watch over the children and for Senor Rodriguez for being drunk. Senor Rodriguez blamed Gabriela for leaving her child to be with the old man's nephew. Gabriela claimed that she was forced to sleep with Nestor in order to keep her job at the house on the hill, but many disbelieved her: she was known to be promiscuous, a mother without a husband. Sanchez blamed the priest for wasting time with his Catholic mumbo-jumbo. Maria Romero blamed the doctor for interrupting the priest. A sour mood settled upon the village. And then the crops failed.

There had been no rain for months. The river that flowed through the valley ran dry. The fruit on the trees withered and died. The dusty soil, from which Senor Rodriguez had hoped to harvest potatoes, yielded nothing but dark clumps, like misshapen tumours. The coffee bushes that lined the slopes of the valley to the south of the village, normally an endless sea of green, spread before them like a yellow stain. Sanchez and the farmers blamed foreigners and factories for disturbing the balance of nature. The Church and the priest, who had wanted to guide the dying girl into the arms of the Lord, blamed the godless townsfolk and the communists in the mountains. Maria Romero blamed *la pequeña bastarda*, the halfwit Pajarita, whom she'd always said would bring ruin to the village.

They called it *el año del diablo*, the Year of the Devil. The villagers hid as best they could from the glowering sun. Dogs gasped in the shade and died in the streets. Cats slept fitfully in the empty barns, so weary of the heat that they starved to death, as thin as weasels. Unable to cool their blood, tiny songbirds fell from the sky like stones from hell, as if they had been cursed, which some believed they had. Only three things flourished in the heat: roaches, rats and bands of murderous crows, feasting on the carcasses of animals that lay dead upon the ground.

The carrion crows grew ever more brazen, congregating on the roof of the Rodriguez family home and especially, or so it seemed, on top of the house next door where Gabriela Aguilar tended to the needs of her daughter. One of the birds drew blood from Isabela's arm, and Sanchez lost an eye as he lay drunk on a bench, insensitive at first to the probing beak of a hooded marauder. And when at last the darkening cloud of birds stretched all the way from the house on the hill to the hovels in the valley, Maria Romero fed her poison to the villagers who gathered around her, with wooden stakes and rusty knives intent on putting an end to the curse by snuffing out the life of the *pequeña bastarda*, whose tortured soul called to the birds as the sun rose in the morning, and swooped through the valley as an owl at night.

When the mob reached the house of Gabriela Aguilar, they were surprised to see Pajarita slumped in a chair on the porch, her head to one side, with drool escaping her lips. Her mother stood behind her. Pajarita groaned softly as Maria Romero approached, and Gabriela placed a reassuring hand on the young girl's shoulder. In the other, Pajarita's mother held a shotgun. The little bird was no longer as the mob remembered her. Her skin was pallid and her flesh was loose. Her eyes were hooded but fierce and dark. Her legs were thin and covered in downy hair, which Maria Romero later claimed to be feathers.

'We have no quarrel with you,' she said. 'We have come for the She-Devil. But we shall kill you too, if we must, Gabriela. So, what is it to be?'

And that was when it happened.

Pajarita slowly pulled herself upright and looked at Maria Romero with furious intensity. The sky above her darkened as the crows began to swarm like locusts, a mass of black sufficient to dim the sun. Then, like a puppet, raised to its feet by invisible strings, Pajarita rose from her chair and looked to the heavens, croaking and screeching like a wounded raven, her voice growing louder and louder, until the mob were forced to drop their weapons and cover their ears. Some said that they saw Maria Romero wipe blood from the corners of her eyes.

And, as if the crippled girl had called to the gods, the swarm of crows revealed itself as a bank of cloud from which rain began to fall upon the earth, at first as a gentle shower, but finally as a torrent of water that filled the empty wells and turned the streets to rivers of mud, washing away the filth that had collected in rancid heaps during *el año del diablo*. The storm lasted for three days and three nights without relief, and when at last the tempest abated and the villagers opened their doors to the world again, the plague of crows had vanished.

The priest reported the event to the bishop, who referred it to the archbishop and so on to the csardinal. It was, they said, a miracle. La Pajarita had been touched by God, and God had chosen to redeem the village from the sins of the faithless and the communists in their midst. The village priest reminded those, who were loyal to the Church, that it was he who had rescued the little girl from the torments of hell to which she would otherwise have been condemned by her mother. The doctor gently shook his head.

Within a year, the crops had recovered, and life in the village returned to normal, except for the pilgrims that came to see La Pajarita, the miracle-worker. She was no longer confined to a wheelchair but remained silent, either by choice or by divine intervention. They called her *La Palomita*, the little dove. Some said that she spoke only to God, and that He spoke directly to her. Many in the village and beyond believed that she was destined for sainthood and came to revere her mother as a vessel of the Lord as well. The doctor, whom Gabriela Aguilar married, was amused by the status accorded to his wife, but pleased that the little girl, whose life he had saved, was now protected by an aura of mystery and acclaim.

In the valley at the foot of the hill, however, Maria Romero skulked in the shadows, brooding over the betrayal of the villagers and the shallowness of the priest who had so cravenly misled the Church. *La pequeña bastarda*, she told those who remained close to her, was an omen of the end of days, a herald of the Antichrist, a vulture that would eat away at the rotting body of the one true Church. Unless she could be stopped.

Hunger

Blurred by drizzle, the small figure clambers the wooden fence like a leveret. From the warmth behind the staffroom window, steaming mug clasped, Douglas watches the boy scramble the final rung and almost fall face-first into the bog of the playing field.

'Big game at the weekend, then.'

Geoff's words join the condensation on the glass. Douglas stays fixed on the boy hobbling across a marbled pitch, becoming more discernible the closer he gets.

'Reckon your lads will lift the trophy?'

The boy reaches the grey block, heaves open double doors, then disappears as if consumed by the building.

'You dreaming of victory?'

'Eh?' Douglas turns.

'All you usually think about.' Wryness percolates Geoff's tone.

Douglas takes a slug of coffee, its heat cascading through him. 'Know much about Marcus Lovell?'

'What's he done?'

'Nothing.' Another swill of bitter darkness. Douglas wonders how much coffee would fill a man his size with warmth. 'It's just… P.E. yesterday. Down he went, injured. Banged his knee or something.' Douglas snatches a Bourbon from a half-empty biscuit tin. Crunches. Crumbly sweetness. 'Sat there wailing. Wouldn't move.'

Geoff helps himself to a custard cream. Chuckles. 'Don't you make anyone wailing do laps around the pitch?'

'Had to scoop him up, carry him inside. So skinny. Never noticed before.'

'You're just used to rugby players.'

'Something about it.' Douglas shudders as if trying to rid himself of a chill. 'So fragile. Like carrying a bird.'

'You're getting soft in your old age, Mr Stone.' Geoff peers accusingly over his glasses. 'Thought you believed in survival of the fittest.'

Douglas's fingers rummage his beard. 'He's a good lad, far as I know. Used to be quite sporty. Didn't know if he was having any… difficulties?'

'Don't worry yourself. Kids go through phases. Leave it to the parents.'

'What if his parents are struggling?'

'They're a decent family.'

Douglas reaches for another biscuit. Then pulls his hand back. 'I guess everyone's circumstances can change.'

Geoff brushes crumbs from his elbow-padded jacket. 'As I said, not your problem.'

The bell rings. A groan. 'Once more unto the breach, dear friends, once more.' Geoff dumps his mug in the sink. 'For there is none of you so mean and base as Class 5B.'

Douglas flexes his muscular arms. 'It's going to be muddy hell for my class, Mr Sully.'

Douglas strides down the crowded corridor, schoolchildren flowing around him. A whistle waits patiently around his neck. E numbers and testosterone fizz, more chemicals than a laboratory. Competing deodorants cloy the thick air against an undercurrent of sweat. Pupils push, shove, snigger and shriek.

'Hands out your pockets, Dawson.'

A scruffy student obliges with a huff.

In his peripheral vision, Douglas notices a limping figure.

'Marcus.' A swift sidestep blocks the boy's path. 'How's the knee?'

Marcus looks up with the startled eyes of a rabbit. Swallows. 'S'ok, sir.'

Douglas inspects him. The black blazer swamping, baggy white shirt, skinny tie skewwhiff. Towers over him.

'Everything all right, Marcus?'

Those small, blue eyes dart around. 'Fine, sir.'

'No problems at home?' Marcus' fair hair shimmies. Feet clatter past. A high-pitched squeal that would trouble dogs. 'Nothing you need to talk about?'

Marcus studies his shoes. 'I'll be late for lesson, sir.'

'Very well. Don't let me keep you.'

Douglas watches Marcus shadow-walking as if through broken glass. Other kids burst past. He'd always just accepted they were of differing shapes and sizes, growing at different speeds. Lanky ones who'd make a sizeable second row. The long-legged and quick-footed, perfect on the wing. Stocky ones for the props.

Marcus disappears from view.

Dinnertime's nearly over, the cacophony of voices and clattering cutlery fading from the canteen. His bulk squeezed between bench and long Formica table, Douglas wolfs a second helping of shepherd's pie. Rich meat, crisp carrot, the tang of strong cheddar in the buttery soft mash. He spots the dinner lady piling stray dishes on to a stainless-steel serving trolley, a stained apron almost covering her floral blouse and flowing skirt.

'Mrs White.' Douglas waves. 'I need a word.'

She trundles across, one trolley wheel squeaking with every turn. Plonks herself opposite, grey curls bouncing. Watches him eat.

'You ain't havin' the recipe.' Mrs White crosses her arms.

'I'm not after that.' Douglas glances around, searching for the right words.

Mrs White snorts. 'Well, I'm happily married so no use you asking me out.'

Douglas's cheeks burn. 'I didn't mean…'

'I'm pulling your leg, dear.' Mrs White leans back with a hearty laugh, her own cheeks rosy. 'But do spit it out. Me shift's nearly over.'

Douglas shuffles, the bench groaning beneath him. 'A first year boy. Marcus Lovell. Does he eat here?'

Mrs White scratches the back of her neck, lips pursing, nose scrunched. 'Think that's Patricia's lad. He used to but not for a while.'

'Is that unusual?'

'Not really. Might have changed to a packed lunch. Some parents have to watch the pennies. Ones that live nearby often go home. Some kids hang about the chippy or sweet shop.'

Douglas's eyebrows raise. 'Can't be good for them.'

'Certainly not as wholesome as my cooking, dear.'

Douglas glances again. Just the odd child eating alone or listening to their Walkman. He lowers his voice. 'Was he on free school meals?'

'Nah, he paid his dinner money.'

'Are there many on free meals?'

'More than you'd think, dear. Heart-breaking some of 'em, coming to school without even a slice of toast. We're thinking of starting something called *a breakfast club*.'

Douglas pushes his empty plate to one side. 'Excellent as always.'

'Good to see a man with a healthy appetite.' Mrs White clambers to her feet. 'And I'll give you the recipe if you want.' She winks. 'Anything for you, dear.'

The changing room is mercilessly cold. Boys on wooden benches pull socks up to knobbly knees and stamp their feet.

'Get a move on.' Douglas paces before them. 'Haven't got all day.'

Dawson approaches cautiously. Hands him a piece of paper. Douglas studies it, chewing his lower lip.

'It's a sick note, sir.'

'I can see that, Dawson.'

'From Lovell.'

Douglas gives Dawson his special glare, sending him sloping back to a bench. 'Could be an illness,' he mutters. A shiver scuttles through him. And a thought.

The corners of Douglas's lips soften as he brandishes the note. 'Thank you, Dawson.'

Dawson looks more startled than when selected for the first fifteen.

A sharp blow of the whistle. In the stampede, the scrap of paper slips from Douglas's grasp and flutters away, trampled under heavy boots.

Douglas and Geoff lean against the canteen's serving hatch like drinkers propping up a bar. Children tuck into their meals, quietened by the surveillance.

Douglas's eyes roam fruitlessly. 'Terribly thin,' he says, absent-mindedly.

'Many of us were once.' Geoff pats his paunch. 'The pounds soon pour on.' A quizzical glance. 'You still thinking about Lovell?'

Douglas watches a girl, slender as a corner flag, nibbling lettuce. And a rugby ball shaped boy snaffling a second pudding. 'Could be an eating disorder.'

Geoff shrugs. 'Possible.'

'They affect boys as well.' Douglas taps his head. 'Psychological isn't it. It's not about the stomach. Could be about wanting to change. Feeling more attractive. Or comfort eating. Or a need for control.'

Douglas imagines the weight of problems piling against each child like a pack in a scrum, pushed further and further back and down.

'Someone's done their research.' Geoff wipes residue from his hands. 'Anyway, I'd better get back.'

He strolls away.

Douglas remains rooted, a myriad of possibilities competing to churn his stomach.

'Just speak to him, dear.'

Douglas jolts upright. Mrs White emerges on the other side of the hatch, crow's feet crinkling as her lips curl upwards. 'Set your mind at rest,' she adds, as if shining a light on his thoughts.

Douglas adjusts his tracksuit. 'How do you stay so cheerful?'

A contented smile. 'Because I enjoy what I do.'

Douglas wanders towards the staff room, the whistle limp around his neck. A crowd blocks his way. The corridor's concerned hush causes his heart to skip.

He pushes past. 'What is it?'

Dawson looks up. 'It's Lovell, sir.' He sniffs. 'He's dead.'

Douglas's heart pounds way more than it ever did on the rugby pitch. 'Out my way.' He barges through. 'Give me room.'

Douglas breaches the inner circle surrounding a ragdoll-like figure spread-eagled on the floor, eyes closed, face ghostly pale.

Douglas stoops. Feels a whisper of breath against his cheek. Releases the air caught in his lungs. Marcus' eyes flicker open, confusion swimming in them.

'You're all right, lad.'

Douglas scoops him up, those bones so slight in his hands again.

'Move.'

His large strides plough a furrow through a field of gawping faces. He shoulders the staffroom door open. Carries Marcus inside. Lays him on a sofa as a schoolgirl might a porcelain doll.

'Where am I?' Eyes skittering. Voice feeble.

'You fainted, lad.'

Marcus sits up shakily. Looks about the empty room as though in a Tardis.

Douglas rests his chin on his knuckles. 'What's this all about?'

Marcus stares out of the window at endless rain. 'Nothing.'

Douglas crouches. Softens his sandpaper timbre. 'You can tell me.'

Silence.

'Look at me.' Their eyes meet. Douglas sees his own apprehension reflected back. 'You're not eating, are you? You're skin and bone.'

Marcus' head drops.

Douglas fills his voice with confidence. 'I can help.'

Trembling, Marcus reaches inside his blazer, pulls out a folded-up poster. Hands it over. Douglas unfolds it.

A photograph of a small African boy. Xylophone of a ribcage. Distended belly. Face a skin-layered skull. Flies circling him. *The child at your door*, it reads in stark black letters. *Hunger, the world's greatest solvable problem.*

Douglas stares as if looking at a crossword, turning it this way and that.

'Sixty million children in Africa go to bed hungry,' says Marcus, his hollow-rimmed eyes haunting. 'For a few quid I could buy him lunch for a month.'

Douglas's brow creases. 'How does that stop you eating?'

'I'm saving my dinner money.' Marcus bites on a nail. 'To send to him.'

'Marcus, you don't have to starve so that someone else can eat.'

'I don't have anything else.' Marcus reclaims the poster, stuffing it back in his pocket. 'And I still have tea at home.' A bony-shouldered shrug. 'He needs it more than me.'

Douglas feels lighter than his frame must appear. 'You're a growing lad. You need three square meals.' He stands up. 'Follow me.'

They weave their way to the canteen. Mrs White is closing the door. 'You okay, dear?'

Douglas gives a thumbs-up. 'I'm fine, thanks.'

'I was talking to the boy, Mr Stone.'

Marcus nods.

Douglas shuffles his feet. 'Any shepherd's pie left, Mrs White?'

Her eyes widen. 'You can't be wanting another portion?'

'It's for the boy.'

Mrs White beams. 'In you come.'

Within minutes a steaming plate of golden topped pie greets Marcus. The two adults sit beside him twitching, as though attending parents' evening.

Mrs White gestures towards the dish. 'Eat up.'

Marcus sighs. 'But I haven't paid.'

'It's on me.' Mrs White rolls up her sleeves. 'There's a lot of mouths to feed. But more than enough to go around.'

Marcus shovels forkfuls of meat, mash and vegetables into his mouth. Gravy rivulets on his chin, colour returning to his cheeks.

Douglas can't help but smile. Feels warmth he hasn't experienced for so long. A sense of achievement stronger than lifting any trophy.

'We can raise money.' He pats Marcus on the back, causing him to splutter. 'In fact, let's make it a school project. A sponsored sports event that you can take part in.'

Marcus nods eagerly, appreciative noises muffled by munching, a satisfied look spreading.

Mrs White rubs her floured hands together. 'See.' She stretches her arms wide. '*That's* why I love my job.'

The Goose Thief

There are not many sky-women, even fewer of marriageable age, so although I was not the most beautiful, I still had the pick of suitors. He was by far the best catch, what with his castle, and his tiny golden goose, but I chose him because he was different to the others. As they swarmed around me and leered at my breasts and made none-too-subtle suggestions of what they could offer, he would lean against the wall, watching and waiting, his gaze warm and steady and longing. Once we were married, he insisted that my magic harp could remain my own.

'You don't want it for a dowry?' I asked.

'No, just you. Always you,' he replied, with calm certainty, as if we had already been married a hundred years.

He was good and faithful to me, and that is the part that wracks me with guilt. You hear talk of women looking elsewhere because of boredom or loneliness or disappointment, but I was happy. He was as I had hoped, as I had expected. So I ticked along, harvesting golden eggs, planting beetroot for the winter, and daffodils for the spring, making grooves in the clouds with my little hoe and sowing the seeds. He would build walls or fix the castle roof, sweep the floors or make the stew. Sometimes he would come out to me and wrap his arms around me from behind, and the dark rumble of his voice would roll out across the heavens.

'My lucky star,' he would say. I would smile and say nothing, because I liked it when he teased responses out of me with the scruff of his beard on my neck, our friction sending lightning bolts into the sky.

One day, when we had been married a few years, I saw

something strange from our bedroom window. It was a great green thing, piercing right through my cumulus full of roses.

'What's that?' I asked.

'Hmm?' he mumbled, his breath a bitter eastern wind; he had gone drinking with his friends the night before. I was sitting in the front room when he got in. He was so far gone that, when he jumped home, he nearly missed our cloud altogether. Luckily he had caught a handful of cirrus and pulled himself up from the edge, but he had been that close to plummeting. He was never reckless except when he was drunk.

'It's a beanstalk,' I said, in disbelief.

'Huh,' he said, finally getting out of bed. 'Must have come up from Land-Below. Tell you what, give it a couple of days, and when it can hold my weight, I'll pop down and pick you some thumb-men for tea. My gran always used to do them with a mustard sauce, back when there were ways to get down. That'll be a treat, eh?' His breath was still rank, so I kissed him on the cheek, rather than the lips, and went to do my chores.

That night, after dinner, he went up to bed, and I stayed in the kitchen to read awhile. My book was called, 'Life in Land-Below' and had been written by an earth-man back in the days when the earth and sky were connected. The author had taken a surprisingly kind view of thumb-men, saying they were not as vicious as some people believed. He had watched them from a distance for some time and come to the conclusion that they were only dangerous when provoked, and more afraid of us than we were of them.

I started thinking about the beanstalk and how useful it might be. There is nothing wrong with leaping from cloud to cloud as a means of getting around, of course. But to be able to go to Land-Below without plummeting to your death, well, it was certainly an interesting idea for a holiday.

I was half-dozing when there was a loud squawk from the goose outside. I ran out to him with a candle in hand.

'There, now,' I cooed soothingly, and smoothed his shining feathers with one finger. 'It's all right.' But as I stroked him my finger met something small and wriggly. I shrieked and flicked it away, and it landed in the cloud with a small *oomph*. I held my candle to it, and it wriggled and turned around and looked at me with bright blue eyes. It was a thumb-man.

'You were trying to steal the goose.'

The thumb-man watched me with wide eyes.

Slowly, he bowed. 'I-I just thought I'd have a look, my beautiful mistress,' he replied. I had never seen a thumb-man in person before, so I was quite surprised he spoke our language.

'It's not for sale.'

'Then I shan't make an offer,' said the thumb-man, looking shifty and sweaty. He glanced nervously at my candle. 'Madam, would you mind not holding that so close? It's terribly hot.'

'How did you get here?'

'I climbed the beanstalk.'

'But where did it come from?'

'It's a long story,' he said and, glancing to the light in the kitchen window added, 'If I could trouble you for some dinner, I'd be happy to tell it.'

Of course, it was unthinkable, and yet I had been startled by the knowledge that a thing my husband had been glad to eat was talking to me. I was curious to learn more about his kind, to understand how a being so small could live happily in the world. So I stooped and allowed him to climb onto my open hand.

'Your hand is almost as soft as your cloud,' he said, looking up at me with his handsome, blue eyes. I shivered and brought him inside.

We spent the entire night talking. I had a hundred questions to ask him about Land-Below and earth-dwellers and thumb-men. He was eloquent and chatty, and yet such a good listener that, speaking to him, I almost felt as though I had never had a proper conversation until then. I told him all about my magic harp, my life, my marriage. We even cracked jokes together.

'You're ever so funny,' he said at one point, wiping tears of laughter from his eyes. No one had ever called me funny before.

'You're the funny one, Master Thumb.'

'They call me Jack back home,' he said. He told me about his home, about his unkind mother and poor cow whom he'd been forced to barter away. He wanted to make his fortune, though he did not yet know how. 'I suppose you could call me a dreamer.'

'We don't get many dreamers here in the clouds,' I said, and I was surprised by the sadness in my own voice. As the sun started to rise, I heard my husband coming downstairs. 'You must go, Master Jack. My husband will surely eat you if he finds you.'

'I'd like to see him try,' he said, with false bravado, then shook his head and smiled fondly. 'May I come and see you again, Mistress Giant?'

'Best not,' I said, although my heart ached at the response. I heard my husband coming to the kitchen door. I held out my hand for him to climb onto and stepped into the garden, dropping him in the cloud where I prayed he would not be seen.

'Flee, fly, Master Thumb.'

He did as he was bid, but not before dropping a kiss on the end of my finger.

My husband entered the kitchen and looked at me confusedly.

'You never came up last night.'

'I fell asleep here,' I said, and he must have seen the dishonesty in my face, for he frowned.

'What have you been cooking?'

'Cooking? What would I have been cooking in the middle of the night, pray?'

'Something smells strange. It smells…it almost smells of thumb-men.'

'How odd!' I laughed, shrilly. 'Perhaps something has gone off.'

His eyes snapped back to my face, and for a moment, I worried that he would be angry. But then he shrugged it off.

'Probably nothing,' he said.

'Probably not,' I replied, and did my best to kiss away his doubts.

It was only later that I realised the golden goose was gone, but fool that I was, I hoped it had merely come off its tether and flown away, not that my new friend had taken it.

That night my husband went out drinking again, and on some strange whim, I decided to dress up in my finest gown and my grandmother's earth-stone earrings and admire myself in the looking-glass. It had been a long while since I had tried to make myself beautiful, a long while since I'd felt the urge. I sat on the end of the bed and thought of Jack, of his piercing blue eyes and sympathetic smiles and kindness and humour. After one night, I felt like I knew him better than my husband. We had certainly spoken more. I found myself wishing that my husband had more pretty words, that he might read more, learn more, pay me compliments beyond 'my lucky star'.

I was wicked for thinking so.

Jack came to the bedroom window and rapped upon it. I let him in, though I knew not why.

'You shouldn't have come back,' I said.

He glanced at the magic harp, which was playing something sad in the corner.

'I…I came to see you,' he said, bowing. 'My darling…I missed you.'

'This is sudden,' I said, startled and suddenly shy. I cursed myself for being so easily unnerved.

'You look wonderful,' he said, his eyes dancing with something so thrilling and happy that I couldn't help but smile back.

'So do you,' I replied pointedly. He looked down at his newly-fine clothes, ruefully.

'It seems that since meeting you, my luck has changed,' he said and, although I knew that he had stolen my husband's beloved inheritance, some stupid part of me felt glad that the goose had been put to good use, that it had given my friend the fortune he sought.

Once again we talked, but I was tired from being awake all the night before, and I eventually fell asleep, only waking when I heard the door swing wide open.

'I smell him,' my husband said, his dark eyes smouldering, his fists clenched. 'I smell his blood. Where is he?'

'I don't know,' I answered, honestly, still half asleep.

'Where's the harp?' I sat up and looked around.

It was gone.

'No. No.'

'I'll kill him,' my husband said, swaying. 'I'm going to...' He strode over to the window and looked out. 'You there!' he shouted. 'Stop!'

I followed his gaze and, in the light from the window, saw Jack standing at the beanstalk with my harp swung haphazardly across his back. My husband ran out of the room and across the garden while Jack started climbing down the beanstalk.

'Don't….please don't! You're drunk. You'll fall!' I cried as he reached the plant, but he dug his fingers into the side of the stalk and started to climb. I ran outside but stumbled in the dark, and when I got to the beanstalk and looked down, my husband was barely in sight. 'Come back, it's too dangerous!'

'He's quick, but I'll get him, love!' came the booming reply. But watching in the creeping light of dawn, the beanstalk buckled under his weight.

It snapped.

I screamed.

He fell, and took the beanstalk with him.

Since then I have taken no company, certainly no more suitors, although there are many who covet this castle. The hole the beanstalk left in the cloud never fully healed, and so whenever I have time, I sit there, mourning what was lost by a moment's vanity.

One day, I swear, I will go down to Land-Below to eat my fill of thumb-men and bring home my poor husband's bones.

All I have to do is weep enough hailstones to make a mountain.

Transitioning

'You pronounce it *mix*. Try it with me, children. *Mx* Rogers.'

'Mx Rogers.'

'Well done. Any questions?'

'Do you have a cold, Mx. Rogers?'

'No, I am feeling better than I have in a long time.'

'Did you go to Disneyland?'

'No. I was absent for personal care.'

'Your voice sounds different.'

'Well,' said Mx. Rogers, pointing at every student, 'a voice is a unique instrument, isn't it?'

The children were confused, but flush with interest.

Serena said, 'My dad has a tie like that.'

Felix said, 'I like your pants, Mx. Rogers. My mom says she wears the pants in our family, but she's not the only one. I have five pairs of pants!'

Mx. Rogers smiled and signalled for the children to gather round. 'I have written a story,' she said, 'for story time.'

The pupils moved obediently into an open semi-circle.

Mx. Rogers read from their iPad.

'Ellie the Eel had smaller fins than her brothers and sisters. Therefore, she might swim off-course and lose sight of her goal. The other eels wanted to help, but they didn't know how. Nigel the Most Unkind Eel called her Aimless Ellie.'

Sarah raised her hand immediately and said, 'You shouldn't call people names.'

Micah said, 'We're all different.'

Elijah said, 'I use fins and a life vest in the pool. If Ellie were my friend, she could use my life vest and swim with all the rest.'

Daniel said his dog had had babies.

Felix said, 'I wear pants and so do my brother and sister.

Sometimes, my sister wears my pants when they don't fit me anymore.'

Mx. Rogers nodded affirmatively to each student and recommenced.

'Ellie the Eel became separated from her brothers and sisters. She was not strong enough to make the climb upstream. The other eels looked on with sadness and regret. They wondered why Ellie was not the same as the rest of the group. *You can call yourself Ellie the Eel*, said Nigel the Most Unkind Eel, *but that doesn't make it true*.'

Eugene said, 'Nigel is not very nice.'

Rajeev asked, 'Is Ellie all alone?'

Mx. Rogers said, 'Yes and no.'

Elijah said, 'A life vest would be just the thing.'

And Felix added, 'I have a pair of pants just for Sunday, but nobody goes to church. They're *just-in-case* pants.'

Mx. Rogers continued her story.

'Ellie the Eel was having a real identity crisis. She needed to know who she was. And she was prepared to ask anyone.

'Early the next day, she happened upon a seahorse who was giving birth to his babies. Ellie introduced herself and said, *Can you tell me who I am?*

'Sammy the Seahorse answered, Well, that's not for me to say, but you certainly are an early bird.

"I'm not a bird! said Ellie the Eel. I don't have feathers and I can't fly! Nonetheless, Ellie knew that eels eat worms, just like some birds. It was all so confusing.'

But Eugene's confusion was elsewhere. 'Can boys have babies?' he said.

Mx. Rogers said, 'Seahorse boys do.'

Sabrina said, 'Your voice sounds different, Mx. Rogers.'

Eugene said, 'My brother got kicked out of the choir because his voice changed.'

Serena said, 'I like your haircut, Mx. Rogers.'

Mx. Rogers answered another question before continuing to read. 'Yes. You can take her at her word. Ellie is not a bird.'

Felix said, 'Boys and girls both wear pants.'

'Later that morning,' continued Mx. Rogers, 'Ellie the Eel met a spiny water flea who happened to be making babies all by themselves. *I'm asking everyone,* said Ellie. *Can you tell me who I am?*

'Scarlett the Spiny Water Flea said, *Well, that's not for me to say, but you certainly are an eager beaver.*

'I'm not a beaver! said Ellie the Eel. *I don't cut down trees with my teeth!* But she knew that eels spend much of their time in water and some of their time on land, like beavers. It was all so confusing.'

Daniel raised his hand and made an astute observation. 'My puppies and the flea babies don't have a dad.' Mx. Rogers approved of Daniel's comment.

Serena said, 'Beavers build homes in the water.'

Daniel said, 'Our puppies look the same, but they're really different.'

Mx. Rogers answered a question. 'Yes,' she said, 'You can take her at her word. Ellie is not a beaver.'

And then the children found themselves in a game of cascading recall.

'She's not a seahorse,' said Chanel

'And she's not a bird,' said Eugene.

'And she's not a flea,' said Serena.

'And she's not a beaver,' said Micah.

'And,' said Felix, 'she doesn't have a pair of pants!'

Elijah said, 'She should really have a life vest. That would solve everything.'

Mx. Rogers complimented the children on the number of details they remembered from the story, and then she continued. 'The last neighbour that Ellie the Eel approached was a catfish. Said Ellie the Eel, *Can you tell me who I am?*

'Cliff the Wells Catfish answered in the form of a riddle. *I don't know*, he said, *but,* he added, *sometimes, backwards is forwards.* Cliff the Wells Catfish knew that eels, like catfish, can swim backwards.'

Micah said, 'How can you swim forward and backward at the same time?'

Hassan spoke for the first time and revealed the depth of his old soul. 'By pointing yourself,' he said, 'in the right direction.'

The children were a little bit confused, but still flush with interest.

Mx. Rogers gasped, drew a big heart in the air and pushed it toward Hassan, and then she finished the story.

'Ellie the Eel realised what she had to do. She propelled herself upstream by swimming backwards. Her brothers and sisters greeted her with joy and cheers. *Hip! Hip! Hooray!* they shouted. Nigel the Most Unkind Eel shook his unkind head. *Who are you?* he said. *You don't swim like the others.*

'I am who I am, said Ellie. *I am ELY THE EEL!*'

Mx. Rogers closed her iPad and answered one last one question. 'Yes,' she said. 'You can take them at their word. Mx. Ely is a genuine eel. There is strength,' she added, 'in difference.'

All the children applauded. They were less interested in the moral of the story. It was somewhat boring and unnecessary. However, each was delighted that the story had a happy ending. Hassan, the old soul, made an observation that seemed to satisfy and offer closure.

'Mx. Rogers and Mx. Ely say their name the same way.'

And then the children enjoyed snack-time and nap-time and play-time. And, at the last bell, they hugged each other and their teacher.

The Despised

When I was seven, there was a kid at school commonly known as *Smelly Eddie*. Eddie lived up to his name – his clothes were always dirty. Most of the time he came to school barefoot, with feet as black as they had been the day before, that is when he even showed up at school. I liked Eddie, he was a good kid with a good heart, and even though he had nothing, he was the kind of person who would give you the shirt off his back if you needed it. Eddie was a friend, and I didn't have many of those. I wasn't popular at school. I was small, shy, not much good at sport – or anything else really.

Most of my friends were misfits like me who didn't fit in or were bullied by the other kids. There was Lance, the Aboriginal kid, who claimed that he wasn't actually black. He'd been born white but had fallen into a fire as a baby and been burnt black. He even had the scars to prove it to anyone who doubted. I had stayed at his place and observed that his whole family were black, and indeed all his cousins – they couldn't all have been burnt in that fire – but I didn't argue the point with him. We lived on the same street, and spent most of our afternoons after school and weekends together – playing backyard cricket with our brothers, making new tracks and jumps for our pushbikes in the bush nearby, or looking for yabbies in creeks and waterholes (which we would always let go again, of course).

There was Darren, the chubby, nerdy kid who wore glasses in an age when no kid wore glasses. We both loved reading and would often spend our lunch hours together in the library. We shared the achievement of reading our first novel together in Grade Two, when we were just six. We were also both totally obsessed with Star Wars and could spend hours playing with our Star Wars figures when we had sleepovers.

There was Pete, the shy kid who came from the Catholic school up the road because his parents could no longer afford the school fees – he would always eat fish sandwiches on Fridays. Strange how, in a school where most kids were poor, you could still carry a stigma if people got to know that your family were poor. Most people probably didn't realise that Pete had quite a sense of humour, once you got to know him. I never visited his home.

And then there was Smelly Eddie. Eddie had come to stay at my place two or three times and was totally in awe of my home and family. He thought I lived in sheer luxury and that my family were wonderful. I found this quite strange, I mean – we were poor! I lived with my single mother in a tiny housing commission home, in a rough suburb on the edge of our country town, in the north of Australia. And I was always fighting with my brother and sister.

Then one day Eddie invited me to come back to his place after school. Eddie had six brothers and sisters, and there wasn't much more than a year or so between each one of them. They lived at the back of their shop, but the living quarters were very cramped. I thought it was tough having to share my bedroom with my brother, but Eddie shared with three brothers – four boys in one room, three sisters in the other. Due to the lack of sleeping space, I could only stay for dinner, and Mum would pick me up at eight o'clock that night.

What really surprised me was that the makeshift living apartment, at the back of the shop, didn't even have a bathroom. They had a toilet and wash basin, but when I asked Eddie where the bath was, he informed me that every Saturday they all went out to their grandparent's farm for the weekend and had their weekly bath out there.

One thing was certainly apparent to me, even though I was just seven, and that was that the leather-goods shop – with leather craftwork homemade by Eddie's parents – couldn't have made much money for them. They were even poorer than my family. They had nothing – and anything they did have was old and outdated, such as the small black and white TV in the corner of their living/dining room.

That afternoon, we took a soccer ball out to kick around in the back yard. After a while, Eddie's older brother came out and asked Eddie to give him the ball. I thought he might want to play with us, but he didn't – he just wanted the ball. Eddie didn't want to give it to him, so his brother punched him in the head and took it anyway and went to kick it against a wall and play by himself. Eddie cried for a while, and I tried to comfort him, and then we spent the rest of the afternoon just wandering around the back streets until dinner time.

When Eddie's father came in at dinner time, it was like an evil presence entered the room. He took off his leather jacket to display arms covered in tattoos, the images all blurred and warped as the skin had expanded with weight-gain. All fighting and squabbling amongst the children ceased immediately, and I felt a twang of fear in the pit of my stomach. Eddie once told me that he loved his mother but hated his father, and I had thought that very strange. Who could hate their own father? My parents were separated, but I loved spending the holidays with Dad at the end of the year. When that man walked in, I realised there was no one in that room who loved their father.

Eddie's frail, unassuming mother quietly introduced me to him. 'This is Eddie's friend, Jerry. He's come to join us for dinner tonight, dear.' People seemed to struggle with my real name *Gerrit*, so everyone other than my mother called me Jerry.

Eddie's father barely looked at me as he grunted some kind of acknowledgement, then sat down in an armchair in the corner of the room and beckoned for his oldest daughter to change his socks.

Eddie's older sister, barely a year older than he, but two grades higher, raced over with a clean pair of socks. She knelt at her father's feet, pulling off his smelly old socks and putting on a clean pair. Even as a child, I thought that seemed odd – that you would put clean socks on dirty feet, without washing your feet first.

Suddenly Eddie's father gave his daughter a backhanded swipe and knocked her to the floor. 'You stupid girl!' he shouted at her. 'Look – you've put that one on inside out!'

I bit my lip – frightened. I wanted to cry for Eddie's sister, but she didn't even let out a whimper. She just picked herself up, apologised to her father, and then took the sock off and put it on correctly.

She got up, still holding her ear where she'd been cuffed, and went and sat at the table, with all her skinny and undernourished siblings, who were hungrily waiting. The man had brought home some Chinese takeaway, which Eddie's mother was in the process of dishing out. There was probably enough there to feed four people adequately. Eddie's mother made sure she dished a generous helping of everything onto Eddie's father's plate, and then did her best to distribute the rest amongst the other nine of us.

When Mum came to collect me, I was happy to get out of there. When I got back, for once, I was thankful for my brother and sister and my home.

I never went back to Eddie's place again, and Eddie never came back to mine. One day, not long after that night, it was lunchtime at school, and I had found myself a seat to eat my lunch, as was normal. I was peacefully eating my sandwiches when suddenly the whole row, where I had sat, got up off their seats and moved, making stupid noises like something disgusting had just happened. Eddie's older sister – I can no longer remember her name – had just sat down on the bench at the other end of the row. If Eddie copped a hard time at school for being *Smelly* Eddie, then it was nothing compared to the absolute hell his sister had to deal with. After all, most boys were smelly – to a degree – it was almost to be expected. But a girl was expected to be clean, and smell nice and sweet. A smelly, dirty girl – through no fault of her own – was simply intolerable, and so the other kids made her life intolerable.

Puzzled about what the fuss was about, I looked around and

saw her sitting at the other end of the bench to where I was sat. I shrugged and continued eating my lunch, with just the empty bench space between us. But the other kids couldn't leave it at that; they hadn't humiliated the poor girl enough. After several comments about her smell and how disgusting she was, and how gross it was that she had even sat on the same bench as them, some of them noticed that I hadn't removed myself yet. So then they turned to me, warning me of my impending peril if I didn't remove myself forthwith, for then I too would be infested with her smell. I looked across at the girl again, embarrassed for her and for myself, then back at my lunch, and continued to eat. If I ignored them, they'd get bored and go away.

That didn't happen.

When I refused to heed their warnings and threats, they started on me – the girls being the worst offenders.

'Ooohh … maybe Jerry's in love with her, that's why he won't move.'

'Do you want to marry her, Jerry?'

'Oh yuk! Can you imagine?'

'Eew! … Now Jerry's gonna stink as well, and we won't be able to touch anything he's sat on either!'

They wouldn't let it be. I looked across at the girl once again. She looked back at me, with a sad look – a look I'd remember for the rest of my life. It wasn't bitter, or judgemental, it was like she understood what I must do. I looked back down quickly at my sandwich, as guilty as sin, as the taunts continued behind me. Slowly I picked up the rest of my lunch, got up, and moved to the next bench. I noticed, with a quick sideways glance as I moved away, that she had simply turned back and continued eating her sandwiches. It was nothing new for her, just another day in hell. A chorus of victory followed me. Even Jerry couldn't abide to sit at the same table as her.

I was racked with guilt for the rest of the day, and that night in bed I cried quietly, but bitterly, into my pillow. I could never let my mother or anyone else know what I had done, lest they be as ashamed of me as I was of myself. For the remainder of term, I distanced myself from Eddie – who just reminded me of my guilt. It wasn't difficult, because Eddie wagged school most of the time anyway.

Then school broke up at the end of year. I never saw Eddie or his sister again. When school returned after the summer holidays, Eddie wasn't there.

The next time I passed that area of town where his shop had been, I noticed the shop had a different name. The family had moved on.

Porch Light

A porch light always says, 'Welcome.' - Anonymous

Sheriff Traynor tipped his hat. 'Good evening Miss Mira. This here is Mr Tom August. He's from one of them big newspapers back East. He's writing about what it's like living in a small town. I just brought him by to say hi.' The sheriff held out a cake box. 'Anna made a cake this morning and wanted you to have it.'

Mira smiled as we came onto the porch. 'Well, thank you kindly, Sheriff. Seems like everybody's droppin' by today with a pie or casserole or some such thing. I swear Michael is gonna get fatter than that lazy ol' rooster of mine.' She held out her hand to be shaken. 'Pleased to meet you, Mr August. She turned on the porch light that immediately started flickering like a trapped moth. Mira turned back to us. 'Michael told me to keep the porch light on so he can find his way home.'

Sheriff Traynor took off his hat as we came into the house. 'You all sit wherever you like,' said Mira. 'I'll just make us some lemonade, and then Mr. August can tell me all about himself. Mira headed to the kitchen to cut up some lemons. The sheriff called toward the kitchen, 'Your porch light needs fixin', Miss Mira.'

'I know Sheriff, but Michael's comin' home tomorrow. I'll get him to fix it.'

'I could send one of the boys over. Michael will surely have better things to do than climb up and down ladders.'

'That's kind of you, Sheriff.' Mira came into the parlor with a frosted glass pitcher, slices of lemon floating on top. She put the tray down and poured the lemonade into three tall glasses. The ice crackled like they were happy to be free from the larger chunk stored in an old style ice box.

'So, Mr August, where are you from?' Mira asked.

'New York, ma'am, born and bred.'

'And you want to write about our quaint little town?'

'I'm doing a piece on lost traditions, ma'am. How some good things people do get forgotten over time.'

'Well, that's a fine thing,' she said. 'You come back tomorrow and talk to Michael. He'll give you an earful. Been just about everywhere, I reckon.'

'That's a fine idea, Miss Mira, we'll do that,' said the sheriff.

We stayed half an hour and then the sheriff stood up. 'Well, time we was goin'. You be sure to say hi to Michael for me.'

'I surely will, Sheriff. It was nice of you to stop by.'

As we got into the cruiser, I said, 'Thanks, Sheriff. Miss Mira is what I always thought a real Southern gentlewoman would be like.'

'She is that.' The sheriff didn't start the car, just stared at the keys, 'You're probably wonderin' why I brought you all the way out here.'

'Not at all,' I said. 'I enjoyed meeting her.'

'I'm gonna tell you a story,' he said. 'Won't take long.'

'This have to do with living in a small town?' I asked.

'It has everything to do with everything,' he said.

I took out a notebook.

'Don't write none of this down. You'll remember it, but you got to promise not to print anything till I say.'

In my line of work, you hear a lot *off the record* stories. I put the pencil away, and the sheriff started telling his story: 'This happened nigh on fifty years ago; right after the government set up the lottery that sent all them boys to Vietnam to get killed.' The sheriff shook his head. 'I still can't imagine makin' boys go someplace they never even heard of, so they could fight and maybe getting killed trying to protect a corrupt government. I was exempt on account of bein' in law enforcement. I was just a deputy then, dumb as a twig on a tree. This was back when Mitch Singleton was sheriff. I was doin' my rounds when I found Michael Englehart hanging upside down from a tree. Been cut maybe fifty times. One cut wouldn't have done him much harm, but with so many, he'd almost bled out. There was a sign pinned to his chest sayin', this is what happens to Commies and deserters. I cut him down and leaned him against the tree. Knew he wasn't gonna last long, so I took out a recorder and had him tell who done this, what they said, everything that happened. He died five minutes later. That recording is what's called a dying man's declaration. Not hardly any stronger evidence in a court of law. Buried that poor boy right under that big ol' tree and went to look for the boys who done it. Walked into Joe's Bar, but stayed in the back listenin' to Ronnie Quirrel bragging.

'"Funniest thing you ever saw," Ronnie was swiggin' beer like they was gonna quit makin' it. "Hoowee," he held up the beer, "you shoulda seen that boy cryin' and beggin', but that didn't matter none to me. I promise he and none of them other college boys gonna ever come down here again; botherin' our women, tellin' us how we should all march on Washington to protest the war. He kept sayin' he was on his way to Canada. Goin' there to avoid the draft, the coward."

'One of the other drinkers nodded and said, "Your country calls, you gotta go. End of story."

'Ronnie nodded his head and downed another shot, followed by more beer. "Damn straight," he said. "We ain't havin' any of them people come down here spoutin' their anti-segregation, anti-war bullshit."

'I walked out of the bar and waited. Hit Ronnie over the head as he was staggerin' toward his car, dragged him to my truck and drove to Hill's Canyon. Asked him a few questions, then threw him over the edge like common trash. Knew there wouldn't be much left of him in a couple of weeks. Then I went and got any of the boys had anythin' to do with the hangin' and drove 'em back to the canyon. Handcuffed 'em to the cruiser and each other. Told 'em I'd already throwed Ronnie into the canyon and they was next.

'"It was all Ronnie," they was all cryin'. Said they was drinkin' and didn't know what Ronnie had in mind, till he blocked the road and dragged poor Michael out of his car and tied him up. Threw a rope over the tree and hauled him up like a piece of meat. They tol' me how Ronnie took out a knife and started cuttin' on Michael, made like twenty cuts all over his body. Then Ronnie turned and give the knife to each one of them boys an' said they could cut Michael or join him on the next branch.

'Stupid kids. What was I gonna do? Destroy the lives of them four boys? Tol' 'em I could shoot 'em right where they stood and pitch them into Hill's Canyon for the buzzards and coyotes to chew on, or they could do the right thing. Tol' them Mira was supposed to marry that boy when the war was finished and he was free to come back. Only now he weren't never comin' back, and that was gonna just about break that poor girl's heart.

'Bobby Taylor tol' me he was right sorry. Said he didn't mean for none of it to happen, that he liked Michael. "You tell me what to do," he said, "and I'll do it."

'I played the tape for them, turned the volume up right loud so they could hear Michael say all their names. "I play this in front of a federal judge and none of you is ever gonna see the outside of a jail cell again. That or get hanged," I said.

'The rest of them boys said they'd do whatever I tol' em' to do.

'"You all are gonna stay here in Fremont and take care of Miss Mira the rest of her days. She got a field needs plowin' or a cow needs milkin', you're gonna see it gets done. An' you ain't never gonna tell nobody what happened. She'd do herself an injury if she knew. I hear anyone in town say anything, I play the tape. Any of you leave town, I play the tape. You understand?"

'They nodded their heads, and that's the way it's been for the last fifty odd years.

'But, Sheriff,' I said. 'I heard Miss Mira say Michael was

coming back.'

'Jimmy Carter pardoned all them boys that went to Canada on January 21, 1977. Tol' 'em to come back home.'

I nodded. 'And tomorrow's the twenty-second, the day Michael would have come back all those years ago.'

'Most days Miss Mira's just as sweet and pleasant as anybody I know. Everyone in town is kind to her, treats her like a lady, which she is. But once a year, she dresses herself up and turns on the porch light, waitin' for Michael to come home.'

'Like a candle in the window,' I said. 'So, Sheriff, why are you telling me all this?'

'I got a cancer,' he said. 'Won't be around much longer. After Miss Mira passes, you can tell the story.'

'No one will believe me without the tape.'

'I'll leave the tape,' said Traynor. 'I want people to know what happened to that poor boy. You're a reporter. You're all the memory some people will ever have, so that's what I want you to do, be their memory.'

'Okay, Sheriff,' I said. 'I can do that.'

Years later, I moved back to that little town, settled down and started a family. The sheriff, Mira and the four boys were all gone by then. I wrote the story, but never printed it. Like the sheriff, I didn't see the sense in ruining the memories the town folk had of all those people. I don't know. Maybe someone else will print the story after I'm gone. I make it a habit, once a year, in January, to go outside and turn the porch light on. Keep it on all night, to remind me of a sweet Southern woman waiting for Michael to come home.

Gnawing worries

Jacob Noakes got off the bus and walked along the dusty roadway to a garden gate. He stared for a while at the flower beds where love-in-the-mist tangled with invading meadow grass.

He pushed open the jammed gate, then his hand went to the back of his neck, which prickled while he turned to close the gate. Was he being watched? There was always someone watching in a country village.

The key the estate agent had given him was stiff in the lock; the door stuck, creaked, and suddenly gave way. This house had been empty for some time. He stepped from bright sunlight into a dim interior, paused and heard a quick scuttling sound from the floor above. Was a window open up there?

The front room was empty, the dim light filtered green by ivy that covered the filthy window. Maybe he'd heard leaves flutter against the glass? But the ivy hung motionless. He examined the bare kitchen, and noted an outhouse beyond the back door. It was much as he had expected: below the spiders' webs and accumulated filth, it was not so different from the cottage he was leaving.

One of those webs caught in his short grey hair as he turned towards the staircase. His chin came up as he raised his hand to brush the threads away, and beyond his fingers he thought he glimpsed some flash, as of intelligent, watching, black eyes. But there was nothing there.

He used his walking stick to sweep more webs away as he climbed the stairs. They led into an empty room that took up the whole of the upstairs space. The ceilings sloped; he had to stoop to explore within a yard of the walls. One small window, a pane missing, and a rowan's leaves trembling beyond it - rowans were like aspens, their leaves trembled in the least breeze. Sunbeams moved fitfully across the floor.

His eyes followed the shifting pattern. Jacob Noakes said out loud, 'Could've been that.'

He pushed his stick into corners where dry leaves had collected. A spider scurried silently to the small fireplace, and disappeared. He stamped, and dust fell, glinting in the moving sunbeams. The back of his neck still twitched.

He pulled a pocket watch from the waistcoat under his jacket. Midday. The pub would be open.

The Jolly Shepherd was a quarter of a mile from the cottage. Jacob Noakes pushed open the door to the public bar and walked into a fug of pipe smoke tainted with a sharper dash from a Woodbine. Three customers and the landlord stared at him.

'Morning,' he greeted them, and asked the landlord for a half of mild.

'Not been here before?'

Jacob didn't hurry to answer until he had taken his first sip of beer.

'Very nice,' he said appreciatively. 'I come from Lower Marcie, over towards Abergavenny. I came to see Fletcher's Cottage, saw it for sale at the agents in Hereford.'

'Fletcher's Cottage.' This came slowly, ruminatively, from the pipe smoker.

Jacob Noakes turned towards the speaker, who held his pipe-stem in a mouth almost concealed by a full beard. The long, off-white strands were streaked nicotine orange-yellow.

'That's right. Been empty a while I think.'

The locals looked at each other, made no comment, looked down into their drinks.

Jacob tried again. 'I was gamekeeper, for Lord Marcefield.'

One of the other customers glanced up sharply and then

looked hard at the interloper. 'You be Jake Noakes. I'll be blowed.'

This man was tow-haired, with a long, pointed nose and a hand that shook slightly as he held it out, pointing towards Jacob. 'He wuz in the yeomanry with me. Sharpshooter he wuz.' The young man spoke fast, almost gabbled the words. 'Well I'm danged. I've not seen you for more'n ten years.'

'Simeon Furlonger.' The name surfaced. 'Last time I saw you, you were on a stretcher. We dug you out after that shell blast. Good to see you.'

'I see you be surprised I made it.' Simeon grinned. 'I wuz pretty surprised too. Still get the shakes a bit. I gardens round y'ere.'

The ancient with the tinned-peaches-and-cream beard spoke. 'Lord Marcefield's never turned you off!'

'No, nothing like that. He's treated me well. But since Flossie died, I can't be easy in the old cottage; thought I'd make a new start. Fletcher's Cottage will do me nicely.'

The third customer spoke to Simeon. 'Yer did oughter tell 'um. I wun't let a pal o' mine take Fletcher's Cottage.' He stood up. 'I gotter go.'

Simeon shifted awkwardly. 'I dun't know anythin' really. Silas y'ere, he knows better'n me.' He waved his hand towards Peaches-and-Cream Beard, saw that the hand shook and dropped it quickly. 'I'd better get on. Missus Sawyer- Brown's a real clockwatcher. I dunt wanter lose the job.' He paused. 'It wuz good to see yer ag'in.'

Simeon was off his stool and out of the door before Jacob could answer.

'War shook 'um bad, see.' Silas coughed and waited.

Jacob smiled slightly. 'Would another pint ease your throat?'

Another pint of mild was soon slipping down past the peaches-and cream facial hair.

'Afore I tells yer what yer be wantin' ter know, jus' settle a question thut's worritin' me. Yer'd 'a' bin too old fer callup, why wuz yer in Yeomanry?'

'Fair question. I was in the Reserve. I went to sign on as an ambulance driver, but the Captain knew me, knew I was a marksman.'

Silas took another pull on his pint. 'Thut'll do,' he said, and began to talk.

'This happened a fair while ago, jus' arter the War. Henry Sawyer wuz grave digger. He lived in thut cottage. Never married. Surly cove of a man – and not prepared to pretend to be anythin' else long enough to charm a woman.'

'He worked up at Manor sometimes, as woodsman. He'd come for a pint of a Saturday. But he kept hisself to hisself. Spoke as little as he could, never a greeting nor a farewell. Which is why ut happened, a' course …'

'Of course?'

'It wuz winter, so nobody wuz out more'n they had to be. An' there wuz sickness about.'

'Just after the war. Spanish flu, I remember.'

'So nobody noticed.'

'Nobody noticed what?'

'Nobody noticed nothin'!' Silas was triumphant. 'Nobody noticed fire wuz out in cottage, nobody seen Henry Sawyer …'

'Nowhere?'

'Thut's what I'm a telling yer. Until Kitty Hawkins died an' Vicar went to the cottage. Door wuzna locked, an' he heard somethin' movin' inside. So Vicar pushed door open. And then o' course he found him. Well, he supposed as ut wuz him.'

'He'd been dead a while?'

'Yers, but it wuzna that. It wuz a cold winter. No, it wuz the rats. They'd bin in an' gnawed, the way they do. Got what wuz easy to get at first, and then they'd gnawed his clothes ter reach more.

'Vicar run out shouting somethin' terrible,' Silas remembered. 'It took a while 'fore anyone could understan' him, and longer 'fore anyone'd go in and see. But us cleaned ut up, had a proper burial. Trouble wuz, them rats.'

'Yes?'

'Us couldn't clear 'em out. Us trapped some, dogs got some, then us put down poison. Thut much arsenic in cottage we could huv cleared up ev'ry troublemaker in village. But even arter all thut, when yer went inter cottage yer'd hear rats. Scurryin' and scutterin' the way they do. And if yer didna hear 'em yer felt 'em, back of yer neck ud tickle.'

'But there was nothing left there for them to eat.'

Silas nodded gloomily. 'Took us a while to work ut out. Longer to believe ut. They be ghost rats. Us reckoned ut all out. Henry must've seed them rats afore he died, seed 'em but bin too ill to do more 'n cuss 'em. But he could cuss could Henry. Yer could say he practised cussin' all his life, miserable feller he wuz. Us reckon he said un 'eartful of cussin' at those rats, an' they be doomed to 'aunt the cottage.'

'Ghost rats.' Jacob Noakes said the words slowly, as if they were the solution to a puzzle.

Silas nodded. 'Live rats in the house be a terrible thing. Yer can feel 'em, watchin' yer, plottin' what they'll do when yer back's turned. Ghost rats are wuss.

'Yer see why us couldna sit quiet an' let yer buy the cottage. Not considerin' as Simeon knows yer.'

'On the contrary.' Jacob Noakes clapped Silas lightly on the shoulder. 'I think Fletcher's Cottage will suit me down to the ground.'

The villagers watched Jacob Noakes arrive in a carrier's van two weeks later. The next day, Mrs Johnson, who kept the shop and post office, walked round with a seedy cake.

Everyone who came into the shop had the same question. Did she see anything? Mrs Johnson reported what she could see was clean and tidy, and Mr Noakes had been very grateful for the seedy cake. She didn't hear any noises in the cottage herself no, and was there anything more she could get them?

Passers-by noticed that the garden was being tidied, and the ivy had been cut back. Jacob Noakes collected his pension from the post office, and dropped in occasionally for a pint. He was polite without being particularly friendly and, as everyone was careful to check, showed no signs of not sleeping well.

Then there was news from an unexpected source. Mike Betteridge was a representative for agricultural feeds. One Friday night he walked into the Jolly Shepherd with the look of someone with news to share.

'Well, chaps,' he said, pulling up a stool to the shove ha'penny table. 'You'll never guess where I've been today.'

'If we guessed her name right, you shouldn't tell us,' called out one wit. 'Not if you be any kind of gennelman.'

'Such a gentleman I've come in here to the public,' said Mike Betteridge. 'But no, you're wrong this time, my friend. I've been over to Lower Marcie, where our new neighbour Jacob Noakes comes from. I dropped in at the Marcefield Arms.'

He stopped speaking and looked round at Silas. 'You don't have a relative that way do you? I'd swear it was your brother in the bar there. Smoking a pipe like yours too. But his beard was a bit …' he waited two beats, 'shorter.'

'Moy relatives be mostly restin' up yonder.' Silas nodded towards the church. 'Stop yer foolery and tell us what yer got to tell.'

'I'll tell you what this person who isn't your brother told me about Jacob Noakes.' Mike Betteridge dropped his voice a little, and his audience leaned in.

'He told me Jacob Noakes was in the pub every Saturday night with his terrier. He never saw the gamekeeper without the dog, since he'd had her from a pup - until the dog died. He said Noakes went almost crazy after that, couldn't settle. That's why he moved away, round Lower Marcie he kept being reminded of her.

'The old man told me things got worse with time, not better. People even started hearing Noakes calling his dog sometimes. The old fellow did say she was the best ratter he'd ever seen. But still – just a dog.'

It was Simeon who said it.

'Good at rat catchin' yer say?'

The men in the bar looked at each other, then into their beer.

At Fletcher's Cottage Jacob Noakes was standing at his open door admiring the clear summer night and enjoying the quiet. After a moment or two he said, 'Alright, then.'

He closed the door and went to sit in his rocking chair, his feet planted in front of him. He felt the familiar warm pressure against his shin and, without looking, leaned down. He rubbed the place at the end of her jaw, just below her ear. Flossie always liked that.

He hadn't heard a rat since his first night in the cottage.

Troglodyte Redux

Alfie has tilted the garage door open so the blizzard can hustle the wood smoke away. Cedar wood mainly, from some old garden chairs. He pokes at the ravening fire with a golf club, keeping it tight to the sealed metal drum; the wedge more effective for hooking rogue timber than whenever he'd chipped a small ball out of the bunker.

That isn't something he's missed this past fortnight, so many walks spoiled, just for the sake of appeasing some clients. Hasn't missed much about working at all.

Hot breakfasts he misses, though. Hot meals in general, especially steak. When the power had cut to his house a few days back, and the freezer was thawing, he'd tried without joy to cook one in the drum. Likewise, he'd wasted a packet of bacon; while he went to fetch bread, it had burnt to a crisp. On top of which, most of the loaf had gone blue.

He has since been surviving on soup and black coffee. He's just boiled a panful of freshly-scooped snow with some instant Arabica and decanted it into a stainless steel flask.

It tastes faintly scorched.

He slips the flask in the pocket of his fleece-padded coat and glances outside between driveway and door. The street conjures echoes of Attenborough voiceovers about polar bears and Arctic foxes and their struggle to find enough food for their young. Only, there are no signs of life to be found in the whiteness. Not even camouflaged. Not even people.

A few of his neighbours departed last week, when the media christened this storm a *Snowpocalypse*. They'd used the last of their fuel to head south. Alfie lacked adequate petrol to join them and didn't have anywhere nearer to go.

Not that it mattered – he was pretty much certain they'd set off too late.

He pictures them jammed in a line down the motorway, like that Ford Transit advert from decades ago. *Backbone of Britain.* Vertebrae fused. Perhaps they are standing between the stuck vehicles, lifting their children to find out what's happening. Through soft-focus snowfall, they look monstrous, like yetis.

Perhaps that is how they will have to evolve.

He feels almost as though he has done so already, in this super-thick coat with fake fur round the hood. He takes his steel flask from the press-studded pocket, has another deep swig, and screws the lid back on quickly to salvage the steam.

He prods at the bonfire, shepherding chair legs back into place. Recalls, out of nowhere, the one chip he'd made that was even half-decent, from the heart of a bunker to a yard from the pin. He'd been so busy gloating, he then missed the putt.

He looks past the smoke that writhes off like a ghost.

In the last report that he'd seen, on the eve of the blackout, the government said there was no need to panic or try leaving the country; anyway, all of the airports were shut. Hunker down, bide your time, and we'll all make it through. *Stiff upper lip* being the general gist.

And maybe they're right, as they have been before. It could just be like a few other years lately, with this cold from nowhere and then suddenly sun. *Snowpocalypse* is simply a media buzzword; it doesn't mean this storm is the end of all things. Doesn't even mean it's as bad as it looks.

It might just be him who has no electricity. The neighbours who've stayed might be tucked up in comfort, pretending that all of these flakes are not falling; perhaps seeking solace in fictive dystopias, which do a pretty good job of distracting from this.

If they are, he can't blame them. Bingeing TV is what he misses the most.

He pulls out the flask and then turns to the window. Icicles glisten outside like diamonds, as enchanting today as when he was a kid. He would sit there for hours and just watch as they melted. Or launch them like spears past the back garden fence - hunting wolves, woolly mammoths, and sabre-toothed cats.

A make-believe Ice Age, foreshadowing this.

He cannot help thinking that increasingly often, despite experts denying this is any such thing. Though we might well be due one; according to established historical patterns, they contend that pollution has thrown it off track.

He accepts that they know more about this than him; they have done all the research and gathered the facts. There's no sense in them lying.

Yet this blizzard just doesn't seem ready to stop.

Another month, maybe two, and how far up the hills might the snowdrifts have climbed? And how long after that until they morph into glaciers? He thinks of such behemoths, nascent and curious, pilgrims in search of their ancestral homes.

Another month, maybe two, and he will definitely have exhausted his stockpile of wood. There'll be no more old deckchairs, no cupboards, no tables; his hunter-gatherer skills will be put to the test. Or at least his capacity for lumberjack work. His handsaw is shamed by its years of neglect, blushing with rust where it hangs on a nail.

He raises the flask for a long final swig, and it has even more flavour of ash. He marshals the guttering flames with his wedge, pressing them close to the side of the drum. He cannot be sure, with this being his first try, but he doubts transformation will take too much longer. Another ten minutes, perhaps a bit less, and the twigs packed inside should be suitably charred.

Then Alfie will follow his heritage, too.

He'll draw vast flocks of planes on the walls of this garage, and herds of saloon cars, and stampedes of trucks. Mammoth container ships, hefting their cargo. Legions of bicycles. Squadrons of drones. Dustbins being ravaged by non-Arctic foxes. Field mice being harried by non-sabre-toothed cats.

Whatever else he can think of.

Whatever it takes to maintain the pretence, the faint hope

that the scientists have got it wrong this time, and the ice is reclaiming the landmass that's left. That the needle won't swing in the other direction, as in previous summers, and there'll be no record heatwave in June or July. That excess CO_2 will not make this snow melt soon, and he'll be able to stay in this cold concrete cave. And he won't have to fret about curbing emissions, or becoming a vegan, or giving up plastic. Nor about hitting the links with his clients, and how well he can chip a small ball out of sand.

The Seven Year Itch

Seeing Red

Ravi had been careful. He had followed all the rules set out so clearly by his family, perhaps a little holier than he would have preferred. He was a kind father. He had a good job and prayed barefoot every Sunday as was expected of him. He drove his elegant wife, Sumaya, to the front steps of the large pale pink temple before he parked the car at the back, because he knew the risk of those high heels, coupled with metres of silk folded around her body that turned her into a colourful moth. Ravi valued being at the table every night for dinner with his children because his father had worked long hours and never managed to sit down with his family on time to enjoy a plate of curry. Because that was all that was ever cooked in his home. Curry. Ravi longed for the exotic cheese of fondue, or the peppery sweetness of Chinese noodles. He wanted his mother to make a potato salad like his friends' mothers, or even try her hand at a Sunday pot roast, instead of the various Indian dishes she presented with great pride, each layered and perfected over years, recipes handed down from her mother who had been famous for her garam masala, the recipe so secret it had never been written on paper.

Ravi was careful, but like all men who think they have just made it out of the woods, he slipped. He called it *slipping* because it sounded accidental, without motive or malice. It also removed a hefty portion of blame, and even though he knew that he was only fooling himself, it still felt easier than the truth. He found that truth could be proud and undeniable in its ability to stand strong, legs akimbo, daring him to a staring contest he was bound to lose.

The first time it happened he was on a business trip. A last-minute signature was needed from a client who required a nudge in the right direction. Ravi was used to these types of people.

He took the flight to Paris with a heavy heart because he knew that Sumaya had always dreamed of Paris, but life had gotten in the way. His job hours, the children, her studies. There was always an excuse. When he offered her a family trip there, she politely refused. He knew why. She wanted to have the dream, to walk the streets with him like in a romantic, grainy French film. She wanted to drink her café au lait in peace, without the crying of her children ruining the soundtrack of the city. He knew that she valued time alone with him, and she was unwilling to compromise that just to have a slice of the dream.

When he arrived in the hotel, it was too late to venture out, and he was secretly relieved because the palette of dining choices in Paris was overwhelming. The pretty waitress in the hotel bar slid the menu across the table and her accent, coupled with a spray of freckles across her nose, made him think of summer, and he momentarily forgot about the rare snowfall outside the hotel lobby window that threatened sizeable traffic jams. The slush by the morning would be unbearable, making him wish he had packed his sturdy boots instead of a pair of stylish calfskin brogues. His eyes scanned the menu, and when she reappeared through a swinging metal kitchen door, his mind was made up. She smiled as she came to a standstill beside his table, millimetres away from his trousered leg. He looked up and read her name tag. *Odette*. How wonderfully French. He imagined how her lips pouted when she pronounced the first letter of her name, the vowel forcing her to look coquettish even if this was the last thing she wanted.

Hours later, after it had happened, he sat on the bed corner and felt the guilt seep into the hotel room that was decorated in pale grey and white, business-like without being too clinical. He ran through the events of the evening again. He had clocked the look from Odette when she had taken his order and the smile she gave him as if she understood the coded message, the sacrifice he was willing to make to appease a hunger that she could not understand. Or maybe she did. Did she know what it felt like to be denied something that over time became almost an obsession? He thought he could ignore the temptation because his society had always warned against straying. It felt like having chicken pox and not being able to scratch. Each moment you avoided placing a fingernail on your skin, was a small victory against the overriding need to simply give in and turn a deaf ear to the clever advice. *There will be scars, darling. You must be patient. It will pass.* Words that were meant to soothe, only maddened him. Being unfaithful was both difficult and a relief all at once.

After he left Odette, he felt lighter. He knew that the emotion was misleading. It was only a matter of time, probably in the early hours, when his stomach would turn against him. It was not used to red meat. It was not used to steak. That was the sin, the thick and sizzling piece of grilled goodness, smothered in *Café de Paris* butter that Odette had placed under his nose, along with a stack of beautifully thin fries.

Ravi looked at his reflection for a moment before he called Sumaya. He hoped she would not notice his deflated tone. Had she been in the bedroom, she would have smelled the steak on him and covered her mouth in shock. She was strict about keeping beef from their children, a meat so holy it was not offered in India, the land of her birth. He was sure she would not be able to look him in the eye if she knew he had taken a knife and fork so easily to his dinner.

The next day he stopped at the Guerlain store on the Champs Elysees and bought her a very expensive bottle of perfume. Ravi was not one of those husbands who fumbled around gift choices. He caught the flitting smile of the sales lady as she recognised someone who needed very little help. He was in and out of the store in under ten minutes. As he pushed the small dark aubergine coloured bag into his satchel, he caught the aftershock of contrition again. He wondered if Sumaya would see the gift as a smoking gun, more evidence of his infidelity. He stood for a moment on the street and looked around him. It was cold and almost overcrowded. The late January sunshine made him think of springtime in London where the light was still too cool to really give depth and warmth to the stone buildings of his neighbourhood. It was a white light, a force that struck each windowpane with purpose but little love.

The trip to Florence was yet another guilt reflex. It was the payment for trying a piece of Wagyu in a hotel restaurant around the corner from his office. His boss had insisted, and it would have been a faux pas to decline, or this is what Ravi told himself as he bit into the marbled meat that he technically did not need a knife for. It was exactly how he imagined the luxury beef would taste. It had a buttery softness that melted into distinct warmth that bordered on metallic, before it morphed into a supple herb aroma that was supported by a thick red wine jus. Buying the business-class tickets to Florence felt like a cheap way out of his own self-loathing, and when Sumaya gushed over the trip, he felt even worse. She hummed as she packed her bag, smiling at him adoringly, clapping her hands softly after he said it would be just the two of them. He was sending the kids to his mother for the weekend.

What came as a surprise was Sumaya's one and only request while in Florence. She wanted an afternoon alone to explore on her own, something she could never do at home, let alone in a foreign city. Ravi suspected she wanted to do a bit of shopping after catching her, eyeing a few stores in the city centre when they'd arrived, so he stopped himself from objecting.

'We could meet late afternoon,' she offered. 'I could pick you up at the hotel bar, like in *Pretty Woman*.'

'I'm not Julia Roberts.'

'You have her legs, though.'

She laughed as she tied a wildly patterned scarf tightly around her neck. The colours standing in strong contrast against her brown skin.

And so they parted ways at the hotel entrance, both smiling at the concierge who had managed to book them a table at a sought-after restaurant the night before. Ravi turned left and Sumaya walked off towards the bustle of the city, the cobble stones clicking under her ballerinas. When she failed to turn around, he felt disappointed despite the beautiful light framing her as her silhouette became less and less distinct.

A few hours later, he found himself on a boulevard lined with small cloth-covered tables and decided to have a drink, an indulgence when he thought about his colleagues sitting at their laptops, even though it was the weekend. When the waiter placed the lunch menu alongside his Negroni, Ravi smiled in acknowledgement. It was just before that time of day when Italians settled down for a lengthy meal, something his office colleagues could learn from, instead of wolfing down tasteless store-bought sandwiches with fancy names. He ran a finger down the card and then looked up at the blackboard that had *specials of the day* roughly chalked. Only one item caught his attention, and while he knew he should have chosen the pasta that was sure to be perfect, he ordered the veal instead. Milanese. The name sounded so exotic, it softened his regret for ordering something so politically incorrect. He sipped his drink and allowed the city to walk by, thinking about Sumaya and the damage she was doing to their bank account. He imagined her running her hands over rows of sweaters in jewel tones and stopping to try on a pair of boots that were totally impractical, but desirable, nonetheless. He could see a boutique owner smiling at her as she stepped out of the changing room in the dress that had caught her eye in the window, and he saw her twirl in front of the floor length mirror before the material came to a gradual stop as she contemplated buying it. He knew that he could not deny her anything, especially after he'd sliced through the crumbed veal that was so tender he barely had to chew. Had Sumaya walked by, she would have closed her eyes in disgust. She had never eaten beef in her life, and the sight of her husband doing such a thing would force her to ignore him, crossing the street quickly to avoid a confrontation.

When he was ready to settle the bill, the waiter apologised profusely. 'I am so sorry, but you have to pay at the bar. Our machine is acting up.'

Ravi smiled at the embarrassed face, following him into the dining area before stopping at the cash register that was plated in brass and decorated in swirls of engraving. Once the bill had been paid, he turned on his heel and, as he was about to walk out, a splash of colour flashed in the corner of his eye. He turned his head to focus on what had caught his attention.

In that exact moment, Sumaya swung into view, biting hungrily into a large burger that managed to dwarf her tiny hands.

Dear Neighbour

JANUARY

Letter 1: New neighbours to Grace - Tuesday
Dear Neighbour,
We would like to introduce ourselves. We are Shane and Danniella. We have bought the house next door. We have heard what sounds like geese coming from your place. Daniella says I must be imagining things. Just because you've got a big garden and some land behind, it wouldn't mean you kept geese. The noise must be from somewhere else. Because, of course, sound travels, as Danni says. Anyway, do let us know.
Best wishes, Shane and Danni.

Letter 2: New neighbours to Grace - Wednesday
Hello Neighbour,
Just checking you got our little billet-doux.
Best wishes, Shane and Danni.

Letter 3: Grace to new neighbours.
Hi, this is Grace.
Yes I have geese. It's a smallholding. And a big garden.

Letter 4: Shane and Danni to Grace - Wednesday (late)
Hello Grace,
We came round earlier, but there was no reply. We thought a smallholding was only for growing food. How long have you had geese?
Best wishes, Shane and Danni.

Letter 5: Grace to Shane and Danni
Hi, about ten years.
Regards, Grace.

Letter 6: Shane and Danni to Grace - Thursday
Hello Grace,
Danni and I are surprised.
We didn't know you could keep animals in a suburban area. Do you have planning permission? You wouldn't have geese if you didn't.
Shane and Danni.

Letter 7: Shane and Danni to Grace - Friday
Hello again Grace,
Just checking you got our note. We haven't heard back from you.
Regards, Shane and Danni.

Letter 8: Shane and Danni to Grace - Saturday
Hello Grace,
Just chasing a response.
How many geese?
Shane and Danni.

Letter 9: Grace to Shane and Danni
Hi,
Three geese.
Grace.

Letter 10: Shane and Danni to Grace - Sunday (evening)
Hello Grace,
Three geese!!! Gosh.
We are both still really surprised. When we looked at the house, we saw no signs of anything more than a big garden. The estate agent didn't mention it.
Keeping geese, we mean.
Have you other animals as well?
Best wishes, your neighbours, Shane and Danni.

Letter 11: Grace to Shane and Danni
Hi,
Yes, I have animals. And birds, chickens, a goat, a pig, a vegetable area, and an orchard. That's what a smallholding is.

And yes, I have planning permission.
Grace.

JULY

Email 1: Adam to Grace
Hi, Grace,
Your big brother Adam here, back from the wilds.
Trust all is ok with you and all your lovely animals. I saw this in the estate agent's ads. . Are these your new neighbours?
Property of the Week
Well priced for quick sale! A substantial detached house situated within this sought after location. Relocation requires the present owners to sell this property within a short space of time, hence the low asking price.
Love Adam.

Email 2: Grace to Adam
Hi Adam,
Lovely to hear from you.
They are indeed the new neighbours.
Obviously the 'we intend to take legal action' didn't turn out as expected.
Much love, Grace.

Email 3: Adam to Grace
"We intend to take legal action"!
What's all that about? What's been going on?
TELL ME NOW, GRACE.
Kiss kiss etc. Adam.

Email 4: Grace to Adam
Don't shout, Adam. It's bad manners.
Love Grace.

Email 5: Adam to Grace
Sorry Grace,
Didn't mean to. Just a bit shocked.
Kiss kiss and stuff. Adam.

Email 6: Grace to Adam

Quick précis.

New neighbours moved in next door where the lovely old lady lived. .

She left the house to all the children. There were so many of them, eight, I think.

They all live abroad, so they sold the house, and the new neighbours moved in.

It was fine to start with, very quiet, I never really saw them, and then I suddenly got all these notes stuck through the door objecting to the smallholding. And that they weren't very happy about it and would like to discuss what I could do to limit the inconvenience to them!

I'm not quite sure what they thought I should do. Apologise for the fact they had bought a house next door to a smallholding, get rid of the animals, or put muzzles on all of them so they didn't make any noise!

Well I didn't apologise, I didn't get rid of the animals, I didn't muzzle them, I didn't do anything in fact, and they took great exception to my 'lack of any positive action' as they called it.

Kisses back, Love Grace.

Email 7: Adam to Grace

Grace,

I don't understand. If they knew there was a smallholding, they must have known there would be animals. I know it's kind of hidden, but it's still registered as being there.

Love Adam

Email 8: Grace to Adam

Actually, I think when it came down to it, because it was a cash purchase, and got a good deal, they skimped on a lot of legal stuff, thinking they could get probably get away without it.

Kiss kiss, G.

Email 9: Adam to Grace

Even more later Friday.

Can you do that? More or less just pay cash, and that's it?
Love A.

Email 10: Grace to Adam

Adam, great news. Mama Cat has had her kittens. Five, absolutely adorable, all different colours. So beautiful. I WANT TO KEEP THEM ALL!
Love G.
PS. Yes, you can do that. For a cash purchase you don't technically need to do any surveys or searches. It's only when you need a mortgage, the lenders require them. But you'd be taking a really big risk. I mean, they could be planning to build a sewage plant at the bottom of your garden, for instance, and you wouldn't know anything about it!
PPS. Do you want a kitten? There's an absolutely gorgeous tortoiseshell girl, or a little black and white one, or a cute ginger, or a lovely striped tabby. Let me know.
You can have first pick. Cute cute cute!
Love G.

Email 11: Adam to Grace

Grace,
Enough with the kittens! What happened about the neighbours?
TELL ME NOW.
A.

Email 12: Grace to Adam

Bother the neighbours, I'd much rather tell you about the kittens.
G.

Email 13: Adam to Grace

Pretty please, Grace.
Love Adam.
Your beloved brother.

Email 14: Grace to Adam

Dear nosey, gossipy, big brother,

Okay okay, I don't know why you find this so interesting. Is your life really that dull?
Well how far had I got? I can't remember.
Love Grace.
PS. Kittens are still adorable!

Email 15: Adam to Grace
Grace,
I'll have a kitten if only to make you get on with it!
You'd got as far as the complaining letters.
Love Adam.
PS. Can I have the tortoiseshell one?

Email 16: Grace to Adam
Of course you can. I'll send you some pics. You'll love them.

Email 17: Adam to Grace
GET ON WITH IT!

Email 18: Grace to Adam
Sorry big bro, only teasing.
Well, it seems they bought the house after only one viewing, paid cash and got the place cheap because the family really just wanted to get rid of it.
Oh yes, I forgot to say, Shane and Danni owned an Italian pizza place somewhere, that had some serious health and safety complaints made against it and then got closed down, after a very public outbreak of food poisoning. There was also a rather large issue with the Inland Revenue apparently, which they tried very hard to keep quiet, but you know how these things get around! Anyway, in the end, they decided not to reopen (don't think they had much of an option about that, to be honest), sold the business, or what was left of it (don't think they had much of an option about that either), and then declared that had always been the plan, and they wanted to 'retire to a little place in the country' (their words not mine). I think it was more probably a case of having to leave the area, actually, if you know what I mean.

Seems like they didn't want to spend any more than the minimum on the legal stuff (or didn't have the cash) so got a friend of a friend to help, and thought they knew what they were doing.

Or rather didn't, as it turned out.

Anyway, after the first lot of letters, I didn't hear anything more. Then all of a sudden, out of the blue I got a letter from their solicitors.

Dear Madam,

We have been instructed by (blah blah) for two paragraphs, and then it went on with some stuff about noise nuisance, offensive odours and health hazards and saying their clients intended making a complaint in respect of Environmental Health issues and get the smallholding closed down, and that I must reply within seven working days or they would take legal action.

PS. Kittens are still adorable.

Love Grace.

Email 19: Adam to Grace

Little sister, don't stop there. You really can string out a story, can't you?

Then what happened?

What did you do?

A.

Email 20: Grace to Adam

Nothing, Adam. I did nothing.

Just waited.

And then along comes a Letter Before Action and a threat to take me to court.

Oh, and a bit about me having to pay their costs, which at present stood at £3700 and were expected to run to about £38,000.

Love G.

Email 21: Adam to Grace

Are you serious, sis?

Email 22: Grace to Adam
Deadly.

Email 23: Adam to Grace
That's horrendous, Grace.
What did you do?

Email 24: Grace to Adam
I sent back a Counterclaim citing nuisance, harassment, breach of peaceful enjoyment of my home and claiming costs and compensation for £41,700 plus accruing interest.
And surprise surprise, I didn't hear anything more about it.
Love Grace.

Email 25: Adam to Grace
Did you tell them you used to be a barrister before you took early retirement and bought the smallholding, Grace?

Email 26: Grace to Adam
No Adam, I have to be honest. I omitted to mention that.

Email 27: Adam to Grace
Nice one, sis.

Email 28: Grace to Adam
Yup!

Growing Power

They told us about the placements in the last week of January. Tegan was bragging to the whole corridor how she'd been picked to work at the stables. She was that full of herself, I had to show her my fist to get her to shut up. She could keep her crappy stables, I thought. I'd rather get lucky like that girl from 'A' wing last year. Placement in a beauty parlour – who'd have believed it? Course, it went out of business a few months later, so that was the end of that one. But I never really set my sights that high. Kitchen work, I thought, that'd do. I could see myself in one of those shiny restaurant kitchens from off the telly - somewhere loud and busy, where there's a bit of banter and too much to do to leave time for thinking.

It's not easy to get a community placement. You have to prove you can be trusted. No one makes you do it, you have to ask. They ain't looking for more people to add to the list, there's too many already, and not enough local businesses wanting to give the likes of us a chance. But the day I heard about it, I'd been stuck in this shithole for so many months, I didn't really care where they sent me.

Then they read out the list.

I stared at the screw with the clipboard. 'You're joking me, right?'

She wasn't from our wing. She gave me this look like, *Are you thick or what?* and repeated, extra slow and extra loud: 'Kelly Harris, Stavemore Garden Centre.' Gardening? Me? I mean, come on.

I went straight down the office to complain. Brian pointed at the line painted on the floor that I ain't supposed to cross and waited for me to shuffle backwards. Then he sighed and raised his eyebrows. 'What is it this time, Kelly?' He always says that, like I'm the world's biggest pain, but he listens anyway.

'My community placement. They've only given me the bleeding garden centre. Lola's got the caff and Tegan's going to the stables. How is that fair?'

He let me talk myself out before he said anything. He's all right, Brian, even if he does sigh every time I open my mouth.

He shrugged. 'Sorry, Kelly, it's not up to me. It's been finalised by the team from 'A' wing. Why not give it a go? If you really can't hack it, you'll have to find someone to swap with.'

'Thanks for nothing,' I snarled. I stormed back to my room, pushing aside anyone dumb enough to get in my way. It's not like they care anyway. No one gives a toss about me here.

Of course Brian knew I'd go in the end. By the time Wednesday afternoon came round, I'd have taken three hours stuck in Tesco car park just to get shot of this place.

Maureen was waiting for me at the garden centre. She looked harmless enough - skinny, dark hair, wrinkles. I didn't realise she was expecting me to haul sodding great bags of compost all afternoon.

'I never signed up for nothing like this,' I told her when I finally caught my breath. 'You want a man for this kind of heavy lifting.'

She laughed. She actually laughed. Her whole face creased up. 'We're all part of the team here, love,' she said. 'You'll soon build up those muscles, you see if you don't.'

I told her what I thought of that, and where she could stick it. Her smile vanished. She chucked another bag onto the trolley like she was lobbing a bag of crisps.

'Why don't you save your energy for your work?' she snapped. 'We haven't got all day.' I could have killed her. Since that wasn't an option, I spent the afternoon doing everything I could to piss her off. Judging from her face when I got back on the minibus, I made a pretty good job of it.

By the time I got back to the unit, I was in a foul mood. The last thing I needed was Tegan wittering on about the stables.

'You ain't never seen nothing like it. The way them horses look at you, it's like they know exactly what you're feeling.'

That girl never knows when to give it a rest. I slammed the door on her and threw myself on my bed. Being with real people – even freaks like Maureen – made being banged up ten times worse.

The damp stain on the ceiling turned itself into the usual hateful face laughing at me. What had I been thinking, to say those things, to act up like that? They'd never want me back now. A hot dark anger rose up inside. 'I hate you all!' I screamed, kicking at the wall.

Feet drummed back from the other side. Someone laughed. I put the pillow over my head and let the tears come.

I waited all week for Brian to drop by and give me the headshake, the one that comes just before the why-did-you-do-it-Kelly talk, but he never did. When Wednesday came round, the 'A' wing screws called my name and dropped me off at the garden centre like nothing had happened. Muscles Maureen must have said something to her boss because instead of shifting compost, they put me in the poly-tunnel, watering and dead-heading bedding plants with two old codgers who never spoke a word.

After three hours with nothing but plants for company, even Maureen and the compost seemed like fun. I spent hours bent over those bloody plants, hundreds of the sodding things, all the same, red and white stripes, purple and white stripes, lined up like kids in school uniform. Beats me what people see in them. I didn't know they were called bedding plants when I started, but you can bet I did by the time I'd finished. I was that bored, I was ready for my bed hours before the minibus came to pick me up.

Week after week, I swore I'd never go back. I always did. I had to. After a while I found I needed it, that glimpse of a sane, quiet world outside this madhouse.

It never stopped raining all sodding winter. Then one day, I stepped out of the bus into sunshine. The snowdrops were finally over and in their place was a blaze of yellow daffodils. There was the scent of something new in the air. It made me feel different – hopeful, somehow. The feeling stayed with me all afternoon. A sense that things were moving on.

They'd already taken pity on me after a few weeks of *death by poly-tunnel* and put me back with Maureen. Someone must have waved one hell of a bonus at her, coz she never said a word about the last time, just smiled and started telling me about the work for the day.

She kept a careful eye on me at first. Then she started to show me what to do and let me get on with it. You wouldn't believe the difference it makes, to be free of someone eyeballing you all the time.

That day in March, we were taking cuttings from the house plants. 'Not bad,' she said when she came back to check on me. 'You learn fast. You've made a good job of those.'

Yeah right. Don't treat me like a child. The words came snarling to my lips, but I managed to bite them back. I was glad afterwards. Thing is, I don't think she was trying to be sarcastic.

Later, as we were tidying things away, I noticed a half-dead plant tucked behind the greenhouse door. 'What's going to happen to that?' I said.

Maureen followed my gaze. 'Nothing. It got missed out of the watering rota. It's too far gone now. It'll have to be chucked.'

Three scaly cactus stems curved out of the pot in thin, yellow claws.

'Can I have it?' I asked.

She looked surprised. 'Help yourself.'

I scooped the pot up and stuck it on the trolley. All right, I wanted to say, I can see it's a no-hope pot of withered stems, but it's mine now.

I hid it under my jacket when I got back to the wing. I wasn't going to let anyone catch sight of it before I'd had time to give it a chance. I went to see Brian, to see if he could help me with a few bits and pieces. He came along with a bucket later.

'What's this all about?' he asked. I went over to the window, pulled away my jacket and showed him the cactus. He rubbed his chin. 'You've got your work cut out there.'

The first thing I did was to fill the bucket with water and put the cactus in it overnight. I know what you're thinking. Cacti live in deserts, right? Keep 'em dry, you'll be doing them a favour. I'd have said the same myself once. But I could see this plant was only just clinging on. It was in no fit state to fend for itself. It needed to be helped back into life.

It's funny how much people will help if you ask. One of those old codgers in the poly-tunnel turned out to know quite a bit about cacti. Loaned me a book. I spent evenings reading up on my cactus, trying to work out how to help it grow. Brian was the first to see the difference. 'That's never the same plant,' he said, when I brought it down from the windowsill to show him four weeks later.

'It is.'

'But it's twice the size, and the colour of those leaves…' He bent down to look more closely. 'Is that a flower bud?'

Wednesday afternoon; a bright, warm day in April. Maureen and I are pricking out tomato seedlings. 'Remember the cactus I took over a few weeks ago?' I say.

'The dead one, you mean?'

'Want to see it now?' I pull it out of my bag like a conjuring trick. Three thick stems spring up like giant spiny pencils.

Maureen stands there, mouth opening and shutting like a fish. Suddenly she drops her trowel, and I feel her arms wrapping me in a fierce hug. I stand there like a lemon, the cactus held in my outstretched arms. I don't know what to do or say. If I move, something might break.

At last, she steps back and gives me the kind of look she

gives her favourite orchids. 'I had my doubts about you, I don't mind saying. After that first day, I told the boss I didn't think you were cut out for this sort of work.'

I feel the colour rush to my face. I think of the way I spoke to her, the anger that flashed out, sharp and dangerous, careless of anything in its path. 'Yeah, well,' I mumble. 'I suppose the place has grown on me.'

'Must be all that compost you've been shifting,' she shoots back and suddenly I'm giggling like a kid, happier than I've been in months.

There's a whole row of houseplants on my windowsill these days. The only one that's hidden is the one I'm growing for Brian. It's a present, to say thank you when I leave. Maureen has the cactus already. She tried to give it back, but I wouldn't take it. 'It's so you don't forget me,' I said.

She shook her head. I swear she had tears in her eyes. 'No one could possibly forget you, Kelly.'

It's not hard, getting plants to grow, once you know how. You just have to find them the right place, somewhere they feel happy, and give them a bit of love and attention. Then you stand back and watch them burst into life.

Migrants

Ruth clutches the baby to her chest. The daughter, Hester, walking now, but only just, clings to her skirt. The skirt is muddied at the hem and faded from too many times in a wash tub. The shawl around Ruth's shoulders reaches below the waist and is indistinguishable from those worn by countless others who are pressing on all sides. It's a mill town after all, and all workers wear much the same attire.

Shuffling her feet from side to side, Ruth stretches up onto the tips of her toes, straining for the sight of the one face who matters. She's assailed by a light-headed feeling. Can't remember when she last ate and her arms ache so. The baby feels like a dead weight, though he's a scrap of a thing, lighter now than the day he was born. Ruth lets her knees give out and lands with a thump on the trunk at her side. It's been banged together with wood that's seen better days. She hopes it'll be strong enough for the voyage ahead.

Ruth becomes aware of jubilation in the air. She frowns. It's as if everyone is fighting off sorrow, the abject humiliation of the final farewell. And this farewell is final. Of that, Ruth is in no doubt. A free passage out of famine is a one-way affair, especially when it's a voyage to the other end of the earth, on a boat that will take forever to get to its journey's end.

'Ruth.' Her name rises above the hubbub. 'Ruthie.'

'Grandma.' Hester's mouth splits open as she shrieks her welcome. A laugh gurgles to the surface. On a swift release of breath, Ruth pushes to her feet, grabs her daughter's hand and reaches for her mother. In the embrace that follows, the baby is squeezed so hard he wakes. With an abrupt move, Ruth pulls away.

'Don't say it,' she says. 'Not a word.'

The grandmother-mother presses her lips together, straightens her shoulders, putting her hands out in front of her as if fending off an attack.

'Liverpool. All aboard for Liverpool.'

A collective moan rises from the crowd. The guard blows on his whistle. He's the pied piper of Wigan. No pretence necessary. Cotton mills with no cotton is the tune playing in everyone's head. Nothing stealthy about savaging the town of its young, luring them away in the name of salvation. Another blast reverberates around the station. The crowd sways, pushing closer to the edges of the platform.

Her husband closes in on Ruth.

'Hurry.'

He hoists the trunk on his shoulder.

'I'll look after them.' He tosses the remark at his mother-in-law.

Ruth shakes her head and stares at this man. Who is he? Two years of marriage and two children under two. What choice does she have? Her eyes follow this husband of hers as he strides towards the train.

Hester throws her arms around her grandmother's neck.

Ruth holds her baby out. 'Your blessing?'

Ruth's mother sags as Ruth gentles Hester away. Ruth's mother staggers and searches her daughter's face. 'Don't look back,' she says. 'Live. And don't look back.'

Ruth pushes Hester up the steps of the train.

Ruth turns when they reach the door.

Ruth searches for her mother.

Her mother has gone.

Ruth stumbles. The hold on her baby falters.

Ruth tightens her grip.

The wheels begin to turn.

Within days of leaving Liverpool, the new-born is thriving. He suckles with new-found strength, gains weight, wails less often when he does, and there is fullness to his cries, determination even.

'Live,' Ruth says to him. 'Do what your grandma said.'

During one of the rare sojourns on deck, Ruth makes her way to the front of the ship. She gazes long at the horizon. Hester tugs at her mother's skirt.

'Back,' she says. 'Back.' She waves an arm towards the other end of the deck.

Ruth shakes her head. 'Look ahead. We must face forward.' Her eyes rest on her daughter's hand with its fistful of material. It strikes Ruth that, while wearing the same clothes as on departure day, the light from the sea has given their garments a brighter hue.

Weeks into the voyage, the roll of the vessel no longer has Ruth bringing up her food. A fiddle, a penny whistle and a harmonica come out, and there's music. Ruth dances with her husband, for she is no fool. On this ship, females far outnumber males. Most of the women are single. The colony is on the look-out for those with the potential to be pressed into service as domestics, wives, or prostitutes – and not necessarily in that order. Ruth watches the man she married, preening under the attention. She gazes upon his admirers and gathers her little ones close, drinking in the envy directed her way. They want what she has got.

And then diarrhoea strikes.

After so long at sea, the smell below deck is fetid. Unwashed clothes. Unwashed bodies. Crammed in. Cramped. Unsanitary. Once sickness sweeps through, it becomes rank down in that hold. Ruth scarcely notices as she pours all her energies into stopping the inevitable. The babies succumb before anyone else, and one after the other, they slip away.

Ruth holds the edges of the sheet together, presses the needle in, pulls it out on the other side, and tugs until the thread has gone as far as it can go. The stitch is firm. She plunges on to the next stitch. Canvas can't keep the water out. She knows that. Neither will it keep the sharks at bay. She knows that too. She's seen the way they follow the boat. Her boy will descend beneath the waves and be snatched up in no time. Ruth shuts her eyes; this will not block out the havoc the sharks will make of her son's corpse. She can see the sharks circling the ship awaiting the next offering from the millworkers of Lancashire. And now her child is the one swaddled in a shroud, his face covered, his body stretched out on the bunk alongside her. Stiffening.

Burial at sea. What mockery. How can they call the dumping of a body over the side of the boat a burial? Where is the grave, his spot in a cemetery to be marked with a cross? She has bound the body in a white cloth; it implies purity, but it cannot keep him safe and warm. This she knows and yet she stitches on, making his little limbs and never-to-be-forgotten face secure. In the needle goes, and out again. In and out. In and out. The timbers creak. The sea is but a few feet away. Ruth knows this too. As she knows about the sharks. Circling. Waiting for their next meal. Her boy.

Many turn their backs on Ruth. This, she can forgive. Her task is hers alone. Yet, she can hear laughter. How can they be laughing? Have they not noticed another of the babies has been taken? And, they're not even half-way to whatever godforsaken place they are heading for.

The white collar turned backwards and the black bible in hand, Ruth sees the man talking but does not hear the words. She watches her husband drop the stitched bundle over the side, heading for oblivion. She sees the fin approach. Turns away.

Ruth is granted permission to walk on deck. The noise of the mills, that once filled her ears, fades away. Now there is quiet. And, far from longing for the journey to end, as she did in those early months of the voyage, now she doesn't want it to be over. The sea has robbed her of hope. Let the sea swallow her up as well.

Ruth grips the rail and leans over the side, watching the boat slice through the water below. She breathes deeply, making ready to clamber up and over.

'Steady on.' Ruth's husband grabs her arm, his fingers digging in.

As she tries to wrench free from of his clutches, the wind catches her hair. Dishevelled strands whip across her face.

'You have to stop this.'

Ruth lifts her arm and points to a fin in the water, moving behind the boat, caught in the churn it leaves behind.

'See that. It's following. Always following.'

'Let it go, Ruth. Let him go. You have to let him go.'

With abruptness, Ruth pulls away, drawing her shawl close around her shoulders. 'Don't you see, he'll be cold down there.' Ruth's voice is edged with steel.

Her husband strokes her arm.

'What about Hester? Remember Hester. We still have our Hester.'

Ruth clings to the balustrade, teetering as she leans over, contemplating the churning of the sea below. She takes in the black shapes beneath the water line.

'They're tailing us. Waiting.'

The husband holds up his arm and turns it first one way and then the other. 'Feel the wind on your fingers, Ruth. The wind is taking us south. We'll be there before you know it.'

He takes her hand in his and circles his arms around her body. The sails in the rigging above fill with air. The ship presses onwards, relentless, and immutable. Ruth slumps against her husband's chest. No tears come. Only emptiness like the ocean surrounding them.

Upon arrival, they are herded into barracks. Spartan but clean. Their trunk is in one piece. Ruth opens it, unsure of what she will find. Packing is now a distant memory. Her mother, who refused to give them her blessing, had been there. Maybe a blessing would have made things turn out differently.

On top of the trunk's contents is a knitted baby's blanket; she's never seen before. One word is embroidered upon it.

'Read it to me,' Ruth says.

'Blessings,' says her husband.

'That's it?' Ruth says.

'That's it,' says her husband.

'No going back then?' says Ruth.

'No going back,' says her husband.

Their voices echo around the void.

No Stomach for it

'How did you get shot?'

I'd been itching to ask that since the early hours. But I was too tired and angry then. Sleep had been elusive; it was hot and the tang of disinfectant couldn't mask the whiff of malaise. Hospitals - I hate them. But when I'd finally tossed-and-turned into a fitful sleep…

He arrived.

His booming voice was disembodied beyond the curtain. 'No, don't be like that...'

'Keep the noise down and turn off that phone - there's people trying to sleep.' The nurse's reprimand came too late; I was already wide-awake.

'Gorra go, they're hasslin' me … don't take any decisions now, let's talk tomorrow - OK?' His accent was Liverpudlian, like mine, but I certainly wasn't feeling comradely. It was 2am, for God's sake. His phone bleeped and his tone dropped: 'Sorry 'bout that, luv. Girlfriend trouble.'

'Try to get some sleep.' The nurse's voice again, followed by the swish of nylon and departing footsteps.

I reached for a glass of water then remembered I was nil-by-mouth. *Please let me have my operation tomorrow*, I beseeched some notional medicine man. After two postponements, I was desperate to get my life back. I closed my eyes, tried to slow my thoughts and imagine my body floating, down, down.

Then he started again. I couldn't believe it! He obviously thought his phone was hard of hearing: 'Jimmy, it's me … Yeah I know I'm behind with the rent, that's why I'm callin'. I knew you'd be at the club 'round this time … No listen man, I've gorrit sorted … No, don't chuck me out, please, I promise you'll 'av it all on Mundee … Can't do it before. Get paid

Mundee, I'm 'ere, workin' nights; all the hours. You'll gerrit then for defo... That's a promise ... Yeah, will do. Bye.'

'Divvy,' he cursed. The voice dropped in volume and the tone softened: 'Can you lend us any dosh?'

'No, me broke man. Sorry.' The response came with a soft Jamaican lilt. I wasn't expecting that. When did he arrive?

'C'mon, you got connections, wharrabout Uncle Billy, he's gorra a few bob.'

'Can't ask him. We don't have that kind of relationship, man.'

'Bur I'm desperate. Landlord's gonna chuck me out.'

'Why don't y'tell d'man you's in hospital, surely...'

'You're jokin'. He'd change the locks, soon as. Bastard doesn't give a shit.' Pause. 'Can I stay with you?'

'Y'know how small me place is. Besides what makes you tink you gonna be outa here by Monday. Dey say it's serous, man.'

'Yeah. Burrit can't take that long.'

'How d'you know how long it take?'

''Cos I do. This time it's gallstones, threatenin' pancreatitis. Before it was ulcers. And before that - in Afghanistan - it was septicaemia. They said the Taliban put dog shit on the bullets. If the shot don't kill you, the infection will.'

'Surely shootin' it would kill anytin' on d'bullet.'

'Exactly what I said. But they had the wound open for six weeks drainin' it. Anyway, you gonna help me or not?'

'I do what I can, but y'know I have nottin'.'

'You might as well go then, if you're not gonna help.'

'Don't be like dat man, y'know I do what I can.'

'Alright, no need for tears, Grandad, I know you do. Sorry. I'm just stressed: me girl's tryin' to dump me, got fired for takin' time off. Now me landlord's gonna evict me. Great eh. Serve Queen and Country – then, when you're no more use...'

'I tort you say dem treat you well when you is shot?'

'Sure, they patched me up good at the time. But they didn't say two years down the line I'd have this. Can't eat, can't sleep, can't hold down a job, or relationship. No one gives a shit.' His tone shifted. 'Sorry Grandad, I know *you* do. It's your birthday Mundee, isn' it?' I could almost hear the smile. 'I'll be there, you'll see.'

'Let's see what d'doc says tomorrow, eh? Get some sleep. Gotta go, I tired man.'

'Yeah, sorry, I'm still buzzin'. See ya tomorra.'

I was suddenly desperate for the toilet, a curse of my condition. I grabbed my dressing gown and pushed back the curtain. An elderly Jamaican gentleman emerged from behind the screen opposite. His brow was furrowed, and he gave me such a forlorn look that I nodded back in condolence.

Next morning The Voice emerged pulling a drip-stand, arguing with his girlfriend on his mobile while heading for the toilet. He was tall, early thirties, well built, with short, dark, curly hair, and heavy facial stubble. As he passed the foot of my bed, he rolled his eyes. 'Women eh,' he said in my direction.

I closed my eyes, how dare he assume my collusion.

On the way back, he paused at the foot of my bed. I couldn't feign sleep this time, I was sitting up with a cup of tea – my operation had been postponed. Again. I was in no mood.

'Heard you talkin' to the nurse,' he said. 'You're from the 'pool, yeah?'

'Right,' I said grudgingly, knowing this would be followed by the predictable interrogation about who or what we might share in common. But I had nothing to do, nowhere to go. So I let myself go through the motions. I was surprised to discover how much we did have in common, including our reasons for seeking a new start in London. But I came in better times and made a life and career here. He came later, couldn't find work and joined the army.

We finally got to the inevitable - why we were here – that's when I asked how he got shot.

'Well, it's some story,' he grinned.

I was warming to him despite myself. 'I'm not going

anywhere,' I said. 'Pull up a pew.'

He began hesitantly, not in his usual bombastic tenor but softly, choosing his words.

'I did okay in the army. Hated the spit an' polish but enjoyed physical activity, so that's what I focused on. Made Corporal by the time they sent me to Afghanistan. I was chuffed to have me own team. They were good blokes and we gorron well. Anyway, one of our planes went down, out in the Bad Lands. It was our job to find it, bring our lads back.

'We were 'coptered to the site; flat, barren tundra surrounded by a wall of armour-plated mountains, scoured and rutted by the weather. It was beautiful in an awesome kind of way. Those Bad Lands man, they're harsh; like a slap in the face.

'As we got close, I could see at once there was no chance; wreckage scattered everywhere. This haze hung over everything. Smoke I thought. To the west was a small village, terraced up a hillside.' He smiled. 'Reminded me of my dad's allotment shed – terracotta pots stacked on rickety shelves. Anyway, the village was flanked by steep wedges of dull purple granite. Ideal for snipers. We circled a couple of times to make sure. Villagers came out of their houses and waved.

'We landed, checked the site on foot. The air was thick with flies, not smoke. The stench tugged at your guts, pulled up your breakfast. Wreckage was mixed with body parts - teeth, feet, arms, legs, bits of torso. And sad personal things - some strangely intact, like the odd boot, sock, or pair of glasses. And helmets, lots of helmets. I thought we were walking through a bog, until I realised it was a mix of blood and aircraft fuel. Horrible. Worse still were the camel spiders. You know about camel spiders?'

'No,' I confessed.

'Ugh, seen grown men whimper like children at the sight of 'em. They grow up to six inches long, run at ten miles per hour, jump up to three feet. They eat flesh. Start by injecting a local anaesthetic, so you don't feel it 'til it's too late. They're not lethal but give a nasty bite; goes septic if you're not careful.

They only come out when they're hungry, so if you see one it means business. They were everywhere, even in the aircraft fuel. You'd think that would put 'em off, but no. I've seen one sprayed with lighter fuel and set alight - it just ran away sizzlin'. They're indestructible beggars.

'I radioed my report to HQ. They said go and check out the village, right away.

'The people welcomed us and the headman offered 'condolences' in his broken English. We asked what they'd seen. A rocket came from somewhere far to the east, they said, from the mountains. The plane limped on for a while before coming down.'

He leaned closer. 'Anyway, I get talking to this woman with beautiful grey eyes. That's the only bit of her I can see, the rest is covered in black. She's shy at first, but her English isn't bad, and we hit it off.'

He'd shifted into the present tense. I don't know why, but he had my attention.

'A boy shows up, her younger brother I think. Turns out he's her son, aged thirteen. She doesn't look old enough. She says the Taliban killed her husband, two years before, for sending his daughter to school. Shot him in front of her and took the daughter. *My son wasn't home, praise-be*, she says, stroking him. He's precious, all she has left, you could tell by the way she looks at him.

'After the lads finish questioning the villagers, I report to HQ again. They say, round up all the males over twelve - deploy 'em to pick up the body parts - then bring 'em in for questioning. I can't help myself, I say: *that's mad, these people are friendly, nothin' to do with the 'plane. It was hit way east of here. If we do this, they'll turn against us.*

'HQ's response is predictable: it's my job to follow orders, not question them. They'll send trucks.

'So we make camp on the edge of the village and cook up some scran. There's flies everywhere. One thing you learn there: keep a handkerchief over your billycan otherwise you get a spoonful of flies.

'When the trucks arrive we start the round up. I have to take the woman's son. She gives me such a look. I try to speak to her, but she won't listen, just goes inside and locks the door. I hang around knockin', shoutin', but the lads start lookin' at me like I'm mad, and so I leave her to it.

'Anyway, we do the deed at the crash site. Then, as we're preparing to load the men and boys into the trucks to return to base, the woman shows up. I think she's come to plead for her son. Or say goodbye. I go to her to explain, say I'll look out for him. But as I get close she pulls this ancient pistol from under her shawl - it looks like something from a Western. Her eyes are blank, like she's in a trance. She says: *Give him back.*

'Next minute the gun goes off; she looks horrified and I'm flying backwards with wildfire in me guts. I hear the return fire from my platoon and look up. She's on the ground leakin' blood all over the place. The last thing I remember, before passing out, is the look on that boy's face - disbelief, then sheer hatred. It still haunts me. One thing I know for sure - someday, he'll take the road to *Martyrs Paradise,* taking as many Brits with him as he can.

'I left the army after that. Anyway, I was damaged goods. Quite literally, I didn't have the stomach for it.'

Too much information

It's hard to say whether it was actually a friendship, but I knew Giovanni well. We talked about many subjects, ranging from world affairs to what was on Netflix; from personal triumphs to profound disappointments. That's the kind of relationship that develops over time between a woman and her hairdresser. The intimacy of personal touch in the safety of the public space of the salon nurtures a perfect environment for a particular kind of close relationship. You'll know what I mean if you're a woman. I suspect men will recognise something similar in their relationships with their barbers. I don't know what goes on amongst the glinting razors, the leather strops and the hot towels, but I'm guessing it's pretty much the same.

Of course, it doesn't happen overnight. There is a trial period where hairdresser and client size one another up. It's not a technical issue. The shape and lustre of the hair after highlights have been applied and the quality of the haircut are secondary considerations. They're not unimportant, but changes can develop over time and little tweaks can be made until both parties are satisfied with the result.

The next stage of the relationship is standard. The hairdresser has to open the conversation. That's the rule, and there are some tried and tested opening gambits.

'Going anywhere nice this weekend?' That's the most obvious one.

'Not really,' you may reply. 'A quiet one.' Or, 'Yes, my friend is having a birthday party. It's a big one with a zero on the end.'

Holidays are good conversation points too. Depending on the time of the year, the hairdresser and the client can look forward or look back.

'How was yours?' asks the hairdresser.

'It was amazing,' you reply. 'A spa hotel in Tenerife, and there were five pools, each with a different theme. It was bliss! How about you?'

'Incredible. Pete and I went surfing in Cornwall. The waves! You wouldn't believe it. You'd think it was Hawaii.'

'And what about next summer?' you enquire.

'Oh well, that depends,' he says. 'We're thinking about the Azores, but we need to find a good dog-sitter first.'

'Mmm,' you agree as fake sincerity rearranges your facial expression; you take care not to say that you can't see the point of dogs.

After three or four sessions in the salon, it is clear whether there is chemistry between the two of you. Giovanni and I enjoyed our initial chats. It didn't seem to matter to him if he covered the same subjects with each customer. The point is both hairdresser and client have to be good listeners, and you have to be prepared to tell some good stories (exaggerated or even fabricated, if need be).

These first few appointments also denote the stage for establishing ground-rules, about how far you and the hairdresser can talk about his other clients. That type of conversation has to take place in resounding stage-whispers of course, to keep up the charade that other customers cannot hear your conversation. You both want to share gossip, but the customer knows there is a price to pay. The hairdresser's code is that he is free to share with others, the same amount of information you wish to hear about them. It's a delicate decision, balancing prurient curiosity against the wish for a smidgeon of privacy. Almost always, curiosity wins.

It helps, too, if each party can intuit if the other needs an hour of silence now and then. That can happen sometimes, and is perfectly permissible if it isn't too frequent an occurrence.

The next stage has to include a mutual sharing of information. Something you don't know about the hairdresser and he doesn't know about you; nothing too salacious, just something personal and mildly interesting. This was the point at which Giovanni disclosed that his real name was Jason and that his vague references to Turin as his birthplace had not been entirely accurate. He had actually drawn his first breath in Teddington, although, to be fair, he had once changed planes in Turin on his way to a skiing holiday.

In return, I offered up – rather generously I thought – that I was now into my third marriage. My first had been to a not-very-well-known actor who also happened to be a drunkard, and I had sent him on his way soon after the honeymoon was over. My second husband was a sober secondary school geography teacher in a girls' school. His greatest shortcoming appeared to be an obsession with the growth of the railways between 1880 and 1930. That is, until he began a rather public relationship with one of his sixth-formers. I found out on our first anniversary, so that was that.

If all goes well, hairdresser and client move on, as Giovanni and I did, to more genuine conversations, sharing amusing tales, swapping recommendations for restaurants and bars and chit-chatting about our everyday lives and relationships. I told him about my husband, and Giovanni cheekily said it sounded as though I had traded up from the previous two.

'Third time lucky, I reckon,' he said.

'Amen to that, Giovanni,' I replied.

In turn, he told me about his husband, the love of his life. Giovanni and Pete had been together for a long time. I didn't know how old Giovanni was, but I was beginning to realise that he was older than he looked. Fifty, maybe. Possibly even more. Giovanni and Pete had both been out and proud since adolescence. They had partied through their respective years of drug-filled youth and both had had numerous fleeting relationships interspersed with some slightly more durable ones.

'Pete said he never expected to settle down,' said Giovanni, 'although he wanted to. Loads of straight people – some gay guys too – think that gay men just want to go out and have a good time. Forever young. But not Pete, and after a while, not me either.'

I gave an encouraging nod, not too vigorously as he was twirling the silver foil around my hair and that was a precision job. He obviously wanted to go on, and he had only applied the colour to half of my highlights, so I knew it could be a long story.

'Actually, we were both damn lucky that neither of us got AIDS,' he said. 'A lot of our friends were not so fortunate. There was a long period when we went to more funerals than parties.'

'So sad,' I said. I thought about patting his arm in sympathy, but I didn't want him to spill the hair tint. Also, I was vaguely aware that the conversations on either side of us had subsided. Giovanni's story was clearly more interesting than those of his colleagues. I didn't want to attract any further attention, although Giovanni seemed not to mind.

'Anyway,' he continued, 'we've been together for so long now. We're as boring as the next couple, and happy that way too.'

'That's nice,' I said. 'So how did you and Pete meet?'

I was certain there would be a good story around their meeting. Giovanni was quite flamboyant and, for all his protestations that the two of them now enjoyed a quiet life, I knew from all our previous conversations that he still liked a bit of glamour and sparkle. I imagined him meeting Pete's eyes across a glitzy restaurant, or maybe they were introduced by the bartender at the Ritz. I knew that was one of his favourite places. Or perhaps it was on a balmy beach fringed with coconut trees. Giovanni liked a tropical beach, even now.

'Well,' he said, 'I was cruising.'

I knew I was right. I had expected it to be somewhere upmarket, like an ocean liner heading for the Caribbean.

Then Giovanni continued, 'Well, I suppose you'd call it more cottaging than cruising as we met in the public toilets at the top of Walthamstow High Street.' He paused for effect.

'Oh,' I said. 'That's nice.' Then we broke the silence that

floated heavily around us with a gale of unrestrained laughter.

'Too much information, Giovanni!' I gasped through our continuing giggles. 'Too much information.'

'Well, you did ask,' he said, perfectly reasonably. 'And I've only just started the story. Do you want to sit at the basin now?' I'll tell you more next time.'

But he didn't ever tell me more. Giovanni died three weeks later. A mundane end, having fallen from a ladder while changing a lightbulb. I didn't hear about his death until Suzi at the salon phoned up to offer me an appointment with someone else.

Although I knew Giovanni well, as I said, I'm not sure whether we were friends. But we were something. *He* was something.

DIY Derek

Your father's approach to DIY is to write a cheque. As a commercial traveller, he's hardly at home.

'Get a man in,' he barks at your mother, every time she frets over a blown fuse or dripping tap when he dials from a telephone box in Barnsley or Budleigh Salterton.

Sometimes the world of industrial pipework commands his weekends as well.

'Your father is a rover,' your mother says, as if he's the swashbuckling Captain Dan Tempest from *The Buccaneers* on ITV, plundering treasure chests spilling with sparkling jewels.

On the eve of your ninth birthday, he sets sail for uncharted lands, never to return.

'That Sandra Bigelow is a trollop,' your mother says.

She gets her hair cut short like Audrey Hepburn and buys a pair of sunglasses from Boots the Chemist in Shepperton High Street. You stay over at your gran's one Saturday, and when your mother collects you, she's wearing a full-skirted red dress with big white polka dots which reminds you of Minnie Mouse. At home there's a man in his shirt-sleeves clipping the hedge.

'Come and meet Uncle Derek,' your mother says.

He comes round the following weekend to replace the spindle in the twin-tub and lop the crab-apple tree which had been your father's favourite.

Your mother chooses some trendy orange wallpaper for what is now her bedroom, and Uncle Derek whistles Sinatra songs while you paste and he papers. He sports a twirly moustache, and sometimes, in the sunshine, you catch flecks of russet in his crinkly dark hair, like glimpsing gold in a forest.

He reckons a girl should know how to wire a plug, so he

teaches you. He shows you how to measure and cut a piece of wood, mend a puncture and oil your chain. He re-strings your Pelham Pinocchio puppet and lends you his back copies of *Practical Woodworking*.

Uncle Derek invariably wears a Viyella shirt with grey serge trousers no longer presentable enough for his job at the Ministry of Aviation, where he works as something called a clerical officer. His Morris Traveller, an ash-framed estate car in battleship-grey, is an Aladdin's cave from which he always pulls the right size of Whitworth bolt or length of two-by-two. Its once-red leather front seats are cracked with brown veins as delicate as lace. The back seats are permanently folded down to accommodate the clutter.

'I reckon they haven't seen a bottom this side of 1960,' he says.

He tells you he knows a rabbit who's not being looked after properly, and you help him build a hutch. The best bit is the sliding door into the bedroom.

'Very good,' you say, when Uncle Derek is finally happy it's moving smoothly. 'But how will the bunny slide it?'

The rabbit arrives in a cardboard box on the front seat of the Morris and is white with grey splodges, so you call her Splodgy. Sometimes you bring her into the hall to slip-slide on the parquet floor and nibble jagged edges along the bottom of the heavy green curtains.

You never visit Uncle Derek's house on the other side of Sunbury, where he lives with his wife, so you can only imagine his fabled tool-shed with its sawdusty floor and ranks of screwdrivers, its pincers and pliers, its coach bolts and six-inch nails, its tins of Danish oil and jam jars of everything.

'Which school do Uncle Derek's children go to?' you ask your mother.

'He's just got the one daughter, Caroline. She lives at a special school. She's very handicapped, poor thing.'

When Uncle Derek gives you a ten-shilling note for your birthday, you walk down to Pedley's, the ironmongers in the

High Street, purveyors of everything from teapots to timber. You gaze at the gimlets and bradawls, the tenon saws and Stanley knives, the chisels and claw hammers, yearning for everything and unable to choose. Eventually Mr Pedley, in his long, sand-coloured shopkeeper's coat, shows you a new type of screwdriver called a Pozidriv. It has a blue handle and comes in a red plastic case with little compartments for its own special silver screws. It costs half a guinea.

'All the sizes you'll need to start off,' he says. 'I'll knock sixpence off, since you're an enthusiast. Ten bob to you.'

Uncle Derek is helping your mother fix something in her bedroom when you get home. You show him your Pozidriv and quote the motto he's taught you: 'The right tool for the right job.'

'Absolutely. Shall we build Splodgy a run so she can go on the lawn?'

Your mother thinks Splodgy needs a companion. But Squareface proves to be a boy rabbit with dishonourable intentions.

'We'll ask the pet shop to swap him for a guinea-pig,' your mother says.

Instead you go to see Mr Pedley.

'I've got an urgent project,' you say.

Uncle Derek has been coming round less and less, but you know how to cross-cut, how to brace a right-angled joint, and how to make a pilot hole so the wood won't split. You have tools of your own, always visiting Pedley's with the one-pound note your father sends at Christmas and birthdays. Your favourite book is the *Reader's Digest Guide to Basic Woodworking* which Uncle Derek has lent you. You're ready to go solo.

The next evening in the garage, Squareface, temporarily accommodated in a tea chest, is watching his hutch take shape when your mother comes in.

'I've left you a roast-beef sandwich for your supper. Isn't it

Thunderbirds tonight?'

You have your head in Squareface's bedroom where the door isn't sliding properly. 'I've got to finish this. Where are you going?'

'Uncle Derek and I need to sit down and have a serious talk.'

Her voice sounds funny, and when you stand up, her eyes look a bit red.

Squareface sleeps well in his new house, but you don't. You lie awake thinking about Uncle Derek inspecting your handiwork when he next comes round.

Veedon Fleece

It's 1965 and you're in the consolation race for over-elevens at your school sports day. Despite adjusting your plimsolls, you don't trouble the leaders.

Wallop School, Weybridge, is boys only. The guests' event is an egg and spoon race, won by a ten-year-old with plaits and a fringe as fair as exercise-book paper. Somebody's sister: Ali or Abby or Abi.

The *Jolly Roger* is nearly back at Penton Hook marina after a hot July Sunday on the sleepy brown Thames. Colin, who likes to be called Captain, steers the gleaming cabin cruiser into the gravel pits and roars his impressively enormous twin outboard engines. Free from O-levels at last, you're at the sharp end with your left arm growing numb around the shoulders of his blonde fourteen-year-old daughter.

Captain Colin yells, 'Hold tight.' The *Jolly Roger* shoots across the water, straight for the bank. Abi screams like a Hammer Film's starlet, and you tighten both arms around her.

Her dad drops the throttle, and the prow sinks down. He swings the boat through a wide curve and gets ready to go again. Abi's head is hard against your chest.

Captain Colin revs the engines and shouts, 'Last time!'

As the boat makes its mad dash, Abi lifts her face to you, and suddenly you're kissing her.

Abi's feet scatter riots of golden sycamore leaves in Magdalen Deer Park, her woollen-gloved hand in yours. Her sage-green raincoat is buttoned and belted, while your navy-blue Civil Defence greatcoat has lost two buttons, maybe three. On the path along the Cherwell, the wind whips her long hair, so you loop your purple-and-white striped scarf around her neck.

Her cheeks are rosy red but cold to your lips as you unlock the heavy outer door to your rooms in Mob Quad, where you've got real milk in her honour. You toast crumpets on paperclips fettled to the grill of your electric fire and listen to Van Morrison's new LP, *Veedon Fleece*, on your Ferguson record player.

'He sounds like a goose,' Abi says, and her laughter bubbles around your sitting room like water from a hillside stream.

Abi and Lorcan invite you to dinner at their terraced house in what the estate agents are starting to call Brackenbury Village, still known by everyone else as Hammersmith. The house is three-bedroomed, all framed posters and Laura Ashley. There's a neat little garden with night-blooming jasmine and kitchen-handy herbs.

Lorcan leaps up to clear dishes, listens attentively, and relates amusingly self-deprecatory anecdotes. You hate him.

You're evidently the spare man for a dark-haired Debbie, who's nearly a barrister. She probably earns twice your whack, but you ask for her phone number anyway.

Lorcan stands next to Abi, his gorilla arm around her shoulders.

'Abigail and I have some news,' he says, smirking.

Abi smiles and touches her fingertips to her tummy.

You feel like chucking up your passion fruit cheesecake.

You spot her at the Chelsea Flower Show, talking away at the back of a roped-off area of the Sunshine Garden, a terrace of terracotta and spiky cacti. She's crisp in a cream linen suit, her hair in a sharp bob, the managing director of her own consultancy, Pollyanna PR, which the maverick Moroccan 'landscape artist' has appointed to make him even more sought after.

You hover for fifteen minutes, but they're still busy batting business at each other. You slip away.

Abi's in the papers. The now-famous Lorcan has been unable to keep it in his trousers. In a no doubt carefully posed picture, in which her hair looks a shade darker, Abi is conservatively dressed, the wronged wife, dignified but hurting, flanked by an unsmiling woman solicitor with a Rottweiler reputation.

Your own divorce has taught you it takes two to tango. You wonder who Abi might have tangoed with.

The house in Henley is redbrick, a Victorian villa. The young man who opens the door tells you he's a nurse. He shows you into a large, high-ceilinged drawing room.

She's only fifty-three, but gaunt. She raises her arms an inch above the neat covers of her hospital bed, her palms open in welcome. Her hair is dull and grey.

'Hello Abi.'

The young man brings tea and indicates that you should pour. 'Abigail,' he says, 'tires easily.'

She shows you photographs of her children, two of each, and admires the few of your ex-stepdaughter you find on your phone. She asks about your work, where you've lived, countries you've seen. She laughs when you remind her of her triumph in the egg and spoon race.

'Your laugh hasn't changed,' you say.

You drift through the afternoon with her in chat and memory. The light is fading when the young man reappears. You understand it's time to go.

'Darling Abi,' you say, quite unable to use the word *goodbye.*

She places her hand on your arm and rests it there as you lean forwards and kiss her pale dry cheek.

'So sweet of you to call me Abi,' she says. 'No one's called me Abi for years and years. You've made me feel young again. Like that day on the river, that perfect summer's day.

You turn at the door, put your fingers to your lips, and blow a kiss across the room.

The Last Trip to See Ernest

Every month, my dad took me to Stanton Hill to see Ernest.

Ernest was the barber in one of the toughest villages around and had been cutting the locals' hair since the end of the war.

What 'e din't know abaht 'aircuts wan't wehrth knowin'.

That's what my dad said anyway. From what I could tell, Ernest didn't know that much. Everyone seemed to leave with the same haircut as everyone else.

I looked forward to our trips to see Ernest. This was where I started *ter lehrn abaht bein' a man.* Whenever we arrived, we'd find a gang of off-duty miners and knackered pensioners waiting for a tidy up, while complaining about everything under the sun.

My dad was a brilliant moaner. He was always *chunterin' abaht this, that an' t'other.* Ernest's customers were terrific moaners too. I was learning from the experts. By the time I was six, I could moan about all sorts of subjects.

It was *fost come, fost sehrved* at Ernest's, so we were usually there for a good half hour listening to the moaning before getting into the hot seat. Ernest's was different to my mum's hairdresser, which was posh. She had to book an appointment. They even had machines for women to put their heads in while they read a magazine. Ernest didn't have any machines. He just had some scissors and a comb.

My dad had a D Reg, duck-egg-blue Mini. As soon as I heard him shout: '*Come on, Nicky, we're off t'Ernest's,*' I'd sprint to the car in anticipation. Once he'd lifted up the driver's seat, I'd leap in and shuffle to the middle of the back seat. That was the best spot for a decent view.

I liked our trips to Ernest's. We could drive fast, as there were no women allowed. And that meant my mum. She liked us to drive safely. I didn't. I liked it when *we went ovver t' speed limit.*

'Are you ready John?' I'd squeal excitedly. *'Ready... Steady... Go... AND YER CAN PUT YER FOOT DAHN.'* That was a sentence I learnt from him. It meant drive as fast as you can.

We lived on Peveril Drive in Sutton-in-Ashfield which wasn't like the other roads. It was unmade, which was jammy for us because it was brilliant for bouncing. It meant that every time we left the house, I could jump around in the back as we sank into potholes and shot out the other side. All the other streets must have been *made.* They were smooth and not much fun. I preferred *unmade any day o't' wik.*

As we accelerated up the road, I bounced up and down, slid from side to side, and screamed with excitement.

While we waited at the junction with Huthwaite Road, my dad usually turned to me and said something like: *'Yer gooin' tavter caahm dahn. I can't be doin' wi' all that shriekin' in me tab.'*

'But when yer a passenger it's much better if yer shaht John,' I explained.

'That's as mebbe but wehrkin' in a factree's bad enough. I don't wanter come' 'om to it an' all. And will you call me Dad, for God's sake.'

'All rate John... I mean Dad.' I always said John. That's what the other men called him if they didn't say *Youth* or *Duck.* Now I'd done it for so long *I cou'n't 'elp mesen.*

Once his instructions had been followed, *'e put 'is foot dahn.* I loved it when *we went lahkt' clappers.*

We always took the same route. We went passed my old playschool, the house where my mum was born in the back bedroom, turned left down the slope, past the Miners' Arms and up the infamous hill to our destination. I knew the way *like back o' me 'and.*

Stanton Hill was full of rundown buildings, muck from the pit, grubby curtains and most of the locals looked fed up. The village pit had three names. People called it Sutton Colliery, Brierley Colliery or my favourite, *Bread and Herring Pit.* There were loads of mines nearby, so it was hard to remember all their names. I'd asked my mum why it had three names. She said: *'Stop askin' silly questions.'*

She told me there'd been a fire underground before I was born, and five men had died. I said it sounded dangerous. She said it was. So, I asked: *'Why don't they find a less dangerous job, then?'*

She said: *'Stop askin' silly questions.'*

Ernest's barbers had a red and white stripy pole outside. It was on the corner of the main road and a side street that was full of miners' terraces.

Ernest was ancient, had a grey, droopy moustache which hid his top lip and false teeth, and a haircut which didn't hide much of his bald patch. His *comb-over* started behind his left ear and stretched across the top, like it was making an escape from one side of his head to the other. On the way to Ernest's, I asked my dad why old men bothered to do that. It looked rubbish. Guess what he said:

'Stop askin' silly questions.'

Ernest wore one of those navy-blue barber's jackets with a pocket on the left breast, where he kept his comb and scissors, and a pair of pockets on his hips where he kept his knobbly, old hands when he wasn't cutting hair.

When we arrived, the chatting, jokes and moaning were in full flow. I liked it when it was like this. No embarrassing silences. We could walk in, take our place and listen. I went in first and sat down behind Ernest so I could watch him in action. My mum said I was a *people-watcher*. It was a well-known fact. I did like watching people.

I told her I was a *people-listener* too, but she said there was no such thing. I said there must be because it was one of my hobbies. I always listened to people's conversations. She said: *'Yer can stop that an' all.'* It wasn't polite apparently. I couldn't believe it. If people spoke out loud, how was I supposed to unhear what they were saying? I decided to listen but pretend I wasn't. That way they'd never know, and I could learn all the information I needed.

Turning to my dad, Ernest said: *'Nah then, Nimrod.'*

'Ay up Ernest. All rate?'

'Like a dog wi' two cocks, ta.'

I didn't know what Ernest meant and wanted to ask my dad, but there were too many men there, so I didn't. He would probably have just said it was another of my *silly questions.*

After learning about the evils of too much ale, how difficult women were to live with, and what a *twat* one of the Colliery Managers was, Ernest finished off his customer's *short back and sides.* I didn't know what a twat was, but I could tell it wasn't good news.

The customer seemed surprisingly pleased with what Ernest had done to his hair. He nodded in satisfaction while looking in the mirror that Ernest held up behind his head. Ernest always did that to prove he'd cut the back of your hair. Imagine having the front trimmed, but not the back. That would be a terrible haircut.

As he settled up, Ernest asked: *'Ote fort' wikend, Neville?'*

'Aah, go on. Yer never know yer luck,' Neville replied, smiling, winking and nudging Ernest with his elbow. Ernest put something in Neville's hand before he left the barber's with a spring in his step. Neville must have liked his new haircut a lot.

Ernest asked a lot of his customers if they wanted *ote fort' wikend*, but he never asked us. I suppose he knew we had everything already.

When it was my turn, I stood up, slipped off my anorak and skipped to the chair.

''Ow do Klondike. A' yer winnin'?' Ernest asked.

It was like men's code. I didn't know what for so just said: *'Yes Ernest. I think so.'* That seemed the safest bet.

Ernest pumped up his barber's chair with his good leg. His other leg was stiff, and he struggled to bend it. It was something to do with having to stand up all day, cutting hair. I bet it wore your legs out. When I was at the right height for him to start, he turned towards the mirror, looked me in the eye and asked: *'What we doin' then?'*

'You can leave it. I like it like that,' I replied, staring at my impressive helmet of bouncy hair.

Turning to my dad, Ernest raised his eyebrows, as if to ask a question.

'Usual Ernest,' my dad instructed.

'So, whadderyer know?' Ernest asked my dad to kick off the conversation.

While Ernest and my dad chatted about men's stuff – the football, horse racing, boxing, growing vegetables and the state of the Labour Party, Ernest went about tidying up my messy hairdo. Meanwhile, I gawped gormlessly into the mirror, past the brushes, potions and cutting equipment. As I daydreamed, Ernest snipped away. He was in charge while the other men who'd arrived after us listened in, sniffing and making grunting sounds. These were male noises that meant they agreed with Ernest.

Ernest seemed happy with what he'd done to one side of my head, so moved gingerly around the chair while asking what everyone thought *abaht' bloody Conservatives* and if they'd win the next election. We all knew *they'd balls it up if they got in again.* Eventually, he arrived at the other side of my head and carried on clipping, while holding court. Suddenly I felt a sharp pain, which focussed my attention. Staring into the mirror, I noticed Ernest had done his best to cut off my right ear. I yelled in terror, blood pouring down my neck onto my new T-shirt. Ernest stopped talking about Harold Wilson before staring at the mess on the side of my head towards the mirror and back again, as if he was watching the tennis.

'Oh shit,' he squealed.

I burst into tears as I thought about my future with only part of *me listenin' tackle* intact. My interest in *people listening* had been reduced by half with one ham-fisted snip of Ernest's trusty shears.

Ernest panicked before realising all eyes were on him. As he pulled out a couple of antique plasters from a grubby old tin he kept underneath his till, my dad trundled over to inspect the damage.

After Ernest had stemmed the flow with an old rag, he re-attached my flapping tab back to the side of my head while reassuring me: *'Yer'll be rate, son.'*

He carried on cutting but this time *kept 'is trap shut* while watching what he was doing.

As we walked to the Mini, my dad told me to *stop snivellin'*.

'Me mam's gooin' ter guh mad when we get 'om, John. I only got that T-shirt off market on Sat'd'y and it's already covered in blood.'

'Dunna worry abaht yer T-shirt, ya pillock. Yer lucky yer bloody tab's still stuck tot' side o' yer 'ead. Yer mother'll not be 'appy that's fer sure... And I wish yer'd stop callin' me John. It's weird. I'm yer dad.'

'All right, John... I mean Dad.'

When we arrived home and shut the front door behind us, my mum cheerily shouted from the living room. 'Come on, you handsome brutes.' That's what she called us when she was mucking around. 'Let's have a look at the pair of you.'

As I walked sheepishly through the door, her jaw dropped. She went nuts, saying it looked like my ear had been stuck back on *by a bungling idiot wi' gaffer tape*. She shouted at my dad. I don't know why. It wasn't his fault Ernest was clumsy.

They didn't speak to each other much that night.

That was my last trip to see Ernest.

Many Happy Returns

I hate customers. I hate them all.
I hate the smiling, lying, never buying,
let me try on another ones…
I hate the can't decide, what's inside,
the other store has more of ones…
I hate the lay away, let's delay,
don't you have a sale today…
I hate you all.
Go away. We're closed.

Store Motto

It is with no small amount of pride, I tell you, that in the one hundred fifty-seven year history of *Highbottom and Atherton,* there has never been a Thanksgiving Day Sale, a Coupon Bonanza, or Store Wide Clearance. We have never given discounts to politicians, celebrities, sweethearts, wives, or employees, no matter to whom they're related. Our bottom line has been preserved for over a century and a half by following the philosophy of our founder, Lord Witherspoon Highbottom, who said, 'If a gentleman has to ask the price, he's not a gentleman.' Aberthnot Atherton, my forebear, who shares the name over the shop entrance, echoed Lord Highbottom saying, 'It is the duty of people of distinction to always pay retail.'

It only took Cynthia Albertson one day to defile this century and a half year-old tradition; only a single day to find the flaw in our founders' philosophy, for, I am sorry to say…Cynthia Albertson was no gentleman.

When she first came into my shop, I was pleased to see a customer dressed in an excellent, if conservative, Ralph Lauren wool skirt with matching jacket. I asked how I might be of service.

'I want to buy a thank you gift.'

'A gift to show your appreciation,' I said.

'Yes,' the woman said. 'You see this person actually saved my life. I suppose it's too much to expect that you're having *a saving-someone's-life Special* this week?'

'Well, if someone truly saved your life…'

'Oh, he did, he did!'

'Then I'm sure he deserves your most generous consideration.' Having deftly avoided the issue of discounts, I guided the woman around the store, pointing out items in several price ranges. Occasionally, she would stop in front of a display and ask the price. At my answer, she would frown and shake her head.

After a while, it was clear that some prompting was required. 'If you could give me some idea what you're interested in, Ms…?'

'Cynthia.' She nodded toward a display and then snagged a pair of Gucci leather gloves that draped beautifully over the fingers. 'What do you think?' She batted her eyelashes. 'Would a man who saved a young lady's life appreciate something like this?' Then added, 'Of course, he wouldn't have needed to save me if it hadn't been for the glare from your window.'

'Glare, madam?'

'I mean, who could see the bus coming with the glare from your store window shining right in their eyes? Just think, at this very moment, I might be lying on the street, attorneys pressing business cards into my limp, unconscious hand, when someone looks up and notices the terrible glare coming from your window.'

I felt my mouth go dry. It was a vision too horrible to contemplate. I saw only one way to avoid even greater unpleasantness. 'Indeed, madam, I believe these gloves are on special today.' My body lurched in betrayal; an entire history of merchandising tradition repudiated in a moment of cowardice and weakness.

The beautiful creature handed me a card. 'Of course, I'll open an account.'

I looked at the card; Cynthia Forester Albertson of the Gold Coast Albertsons; one of the oldest, wealthiest families in Chicago, and I had given her a discount!

In resignation I asked, 'To whom would madam like the gloves sent?'

'I don't know his name,' confessed Cynthia shyly, 'but he lives at 1914 Sedgwick. You see, I followed him.'

I hoped to put the morning's unpleasantness behind me. However, later that afternoon, a tall, average looking man, wearing scuffed Red Wing boots and a torn denim jacket, came into the store. I was stunned when he pulled out a pair of Gucci gloves and thumped them on the counter.

'I want to return these.'

'Return?' I croaked. In all of retail sales, returns are the most upsetting. There's so little profit in them. 'Was there a problem? The colour? The size perhaps?'

'They fit okay. I just can't take 'em.'

I was forced to face the situation squarely, 'You are the gentleman who saved the young woman's life?'

'I didn't do that much, and I sure don't want nothin' for it. Would you take these and return the money to…whatever her name is.'

'Albertson sir. I could look up her phone number if you would like to speak to her.'

'Nope. That's one person I never want to talk to again, ever.'

'Ah,' I said, 'Perhaps you could accept the gloves in the spirit they were given.'

The man looked at me. 'Are you kidding? She's a complete ditz: ear buds plugged in, texting, crossing the street without looking. You can't accept presents from empty-headed women who don't look where they're going, can you?'

'I suppose not,' I said dispiritedly. Personally, I felt expensive tokens of appreciation were always appropriate. I mean, how long would we be in business if husbands and wives didn't buy guilt-ridden gifts for each other? Sadly, I took the gloves and sent the credit slip to Ms. Albertson's Gold Coast address.

Two days later Ms. Albertson returned. 'Miss Cynthia,' I said insincerely, 'how nice to see you again.'

'You said he'd like the gloves,' she fumed.

'It's safe to say the gloves were not in keeping with the gentleman's general sense of fashion.'

'You met him. So you can tell me what he'd like.'

'Might I suggest a pair of pliers.'

'No,' Cynthia said firmly, spying a display by Louis Vuitton. 'He can't say no to a briefcase.'

'I don't believe that item reflects the gentlemen's…'

'The most expensive one you've got.'

'But madam,' I said.

'Please put this on my account…with my usual discount,' she said and stormed out.

The next morning, the young man returned. 'This is harassment,' he yelled, slamming the case on the counter. Then he too, stormed out.

I sent the credit receipt to Ms. Cynthia and began downing shots of brandy, waiting for the inevitable to become evitable.

The next morning, Ms. Cynthia was waiting impatiently for me to open the shop. She pulled the return receipt from her purse. 'This is absurd!' she railed. 'I'm not going to let some brutish low-life throw my presents back in my face!' Cynthia looked around and strode toward the overcoats. 'What size would you say he is?'

'A forty-two regular,' I said.

'More like a forty-two long.' She grabbed a coat and placed

it on the counter, 'Put this on my account.' She raised her head. 'With my usual discount.'

I nodded dumbly and prepared the cashmere overcoat for delivery.

The phone rang two hours later. 'This is David Melhane,' said the voice. 'I'm the person that crazy woman keeps sending things to.'

'Yes, Mr. Melhane, I remember.'

'You've got to get her to stop sending me stuff. I'm a cable installer for Christ's sake. The guys would laugh themselves sick if they saw me in this thing.'

'Wouldn't it be simpler to just accept one of Miss Cynthia's gifts?'

'OK, I'll come in and choose something, but I'm bringing back the coat. I tried it on. I look like Al Capone.'

Mr. Melhane had the coat back within the hour. He looked around without interest.

A thought occurred to what little was left of my brain. 'Does the gentleman have any recreational activities?'

'You mean like a hobby? I hurt my knee playing ball, so now all I do is a little hunting and fishing.'

I brought out a catalogue. 'Of course we don't have any of these in stock, but what do you think?'

'Melhane looked at the picture. 'Those are nice. Expensive, huh?'

'Very,' I said.

'Good,' he said with some vindictiveness. 'Order one up.'

I did so and sent the $14,000 bill to the Albertson address indicating that Mr. Melhane had returned the coat and chosen a custom fitted Purdy shotgun instead.

The next day, I saw Miss Cynthia striding purposefully toward my shop. I felt a sharp pain in my chest and thanked that supreme store manager of us all for choosing the moment of my demise so propitiously.

Cynthia entered, eyes blazing. 'Mr. Atherton,' she said

grinding her teeth. 'Your name is the same as the one engraved above your shop?'

'It is,' I said, sadly noting the symptoms of my cardiac arrest receding.

'Since when does a reputable establishment like yours, blithely charge customers' accounts without their permission?'

'But Ms. Albertson,' I cried. 'You were so adamant about finding a gift for Mr. Melhane.'

Cynthia's voice began to crack, her eyes brimming with tears. 'I could afford the first few things,' she sniffled. 'I mean, look at him, just a dolt in jeans and a hard hat.'

'Ms. Albertson!' I said, aghast.

'It's not Albertson,' she wailed. 'It's McTravers, Cindy McTravers!'

By now I was wailing too. 'But the bills were all paid!'

'I'm Mrs. Albertson's personal assistant. I paid for the gifts out of my savings, but if she found out I used her name to buy things, I don't know what she'd do.'

'Personal assistant?' I quailed. 'As in social secretary?'

She nodded. 'He made me so mad. I mean, okay, it was stupid walking into the street without looking, but when he grabbed me, I thought he was a purse snatcher, and I said some horrible things, and then when I saw the bus, I felt so stupid, but he walked away before I could thank him. He was…' tears were coming down her face in a steady stream now.

I finished the sentence for her: 'A gentleman?'

Cynthia nodded, 'Even with the stupid jeans and hard hat.'

'Well,' I said, 'I think it best that you and I sit down and have a nice cup of tea.'

'Tea?' croaked Cynthia, 'You want to drink tea at a time like this?'

'Any country that does not have tea in the morning is quite uncivilized, don't you think?'

I was just pouring a second cup when David Melhane stormed into the shop. 'You've got to cancel that order,' he barked.

Cynthia burst out of her chair. 'Don't you dare!'

Recognition flashed on Melhane's face. 'I do dare! I'm not taking anything from you!'

'That's because you're a stubborn, prideful, classless, clod; a compulsive macho type who wouldn't know anything nice if it hit him in the face.'

'Well, at least I'm not some stuck-up, male-phobic, rich-bitch female who thinks she can shove people around just because she's got a lot of money!'

I decided it was time to make a graceful exit. I turned the 'closed' sign in the window and locked the door. I presumed the hostilities would take half an hour; enough time for a triple espresso and a croissant.

I returned to the shop just as David Melhane and Miss Cynthia were crossing the street, her head resting on his shoulder.

I tore up Miss Cynthia's receipts, cancelled the order with Purdy and thought about renting out canoes in Wisconsin.

I opened the new store a few months ago. *Crazy Al's Discount Warehouse.* You've probably seen the ad. I wrote the copy myself:

'CRAZY AL's DISCOUNT WAREHOUSE'
Don't even ask where we get such GREAT brand-name
shoes, suits, dresses and accessories. And you ABSOLUTEY
do not want to know how we can sell them at such CRAZY prices.
CRAZY AL's…
Open all day and all night, but you better get here quick.
With customers like you taking advantage of me,
there's no way I can stay in business.'

What do you think? A bit much? Last year I would have agreed with you. Still, things have been going rather well. In fact, my accountant says, I should be able to buy that villa in Tuscany much sooner than anticipated.

August

Amal is in love with the city. All of it - streets and steps and steeples, roofs and rooms and routes, doors and domes and distances - is printed on her mind like the face of an old friend. Amal loves the cool, clear river which cuts through Munich. The river holds islands peppered with smooth stones. When it's hot, she wades through the current, spreads a blanket and reads in the sun, her body turning a richer shade of brown with each passing day. Pleasure is warmth and water and words.

Fruit and coffee for breakfast. Figs are a remarkably lusty fruit Amal thinks as she bites into the soft flesh. It's her last full day here in the city. This morning she cast the kitchen windows open and let the breeze kiss her face. And now she sits, takes a sip of coffee, turns the page of her book, places the mug on the table where it rests, heavy and white, a clean tooth.

The apartment is small and functional. Each year Amal considers booking a different place but finds it impossible. This is the home she rented during her year abroad, the first time she lived on her own, the door she shut every morning before descending the stairs and throwing herself into the arms of another day spent studying at the university, drinking lemonade in the English Garden, or reading by the riverbank. A routine she repeats now, turning the key in the lock three times.

Mariahilfplatz is emptier than she has ever seen it. Shopkeepers doze on stools by their wares: bread and eggs, baskets filled with root vegetables, fat wheels of cheese, sausages strung up like traitors. The air is scented by the breeze rippling past a stall selling flowers: pinks and dahlias, zinnias and cosmos and bee balm, all held together with brightly coloured ribbons. Amal bends and smells as a butterfly lands to rest its wings on the pistil of an orchid.

The glass front of the Neue Pinakothek glitters in the sun. She purchases a ticket from the attendant, who is handsome in a clumsy manner, the bridge of his nose broken into a kink. The museum is almost empty. A private viewing. No need for a map, she treads the familiar course to a painting she has seen countless times, a painting which has become part of a personal ritual, part of her own body. A vase catches the light and holds sunflowers, their heads heavy with gold, princes unable to bear the weight of the crown, bodies on the verge of collapse. Ochre, brass, honey: the brush strokes euphoric and violent, threatening to burst open, to break every boundary, to smash the thin line of the vase, to blur petal and stem, to gash the canvas and spill out, marking the frame, the wall, the air. Uncontainable joy. A fleeting blush of summer forever in full bloom. Never wilting, never fading.

The flowers are inked on her skin. Each night, as she strips to wash, Amal catches sight of the tattoo on her thigh; no more than an outline, a spray of petals sustaining her until she stands in front of the painting again and brims with a feeling whose name she dare not speak for fear of it being ridiculed, for fear of trying to enclose that which is so vital, so without limits: *ecstasy*.

Guilt swells in her chest. Would it hurt to resist her annual pilgrimage this once? Well, it might not be 'this once'. Who knows what the coming months might bring. When the first news of the virus broke, Amal - a firm believer in the twin virtues of optimism and practicality - thought the disease would die out before reaching England. Surely no worse than bird flu or swine flu or all the other beasts of burden the tabloids use to stoke panic and sell papers. When the schools closed, she tackled the issue head-on, ensuring all St. Ambrose students had access to digital lessons. This, she overheard her mother shout down the phone, was *the kind of behaviour that will lead my daughter to be the youngest Muslim headteacher in England, inshallah.* When the politicians introduced last-minute rules and left Amal alone during Eid, she grimaced and capitulated, tears hitting the mat as she said her prayers.

Everything taken, everything lost. And so a fortnight ago, with Germany listed on the travel corridor, she booked her flights and rang Mrs Hoffmann about the apartment.

Amal shakes her head. She's vowed to leave all thoughts of the virus at home. A week without worries. Waking, eating, reading, bathing, sleeping: alone. No mother asking about the latest changes to the regulations. No students claiming a bad connection at the precise moment she mentions their homework is overdue. No friends repeating *how lucky you are to have so much time off* before she drives home to plan lessons, mark assignments and host meetings with parents asking what, exactly, their fees are being spent on if the building remains shut and the clubs cancelled.

The heat outside appears like a memory. Everything blue and green and blossoming. How the city transformed her. As a young woman, Amal felt the need to fasten characteristics to herself like rosettes, to announce her qualities, to have hard, definite edges. She frequently refused the opportunity to strike out, fearing she would betray this flinty sense of self. But, as fruit ripens, time brings softness. Loosed from England and rid of her own expectations, Munich allowed her to become a constellation of interests - some bright, some long dead, their faded light appearing through the flicker of memory. She used the city as a telescope to view her life at home, enjoyed the vagaries of distance, the ability to be multiple and contradictory and undecided. Now resting, now dancing.

Munich had become her nuptials. The meeting between one moment and another. The point at which Amal realised life could be transcendent. Throughout her teenage years, she knuckled down, showed a steely commitment to success. At university, she never stopped: editor of the student newspaper, head of the netball team, a standout debater. Her own sculptor, carving the future from stone. And then came Munich, the empty days bringing different rewards, knowledge not found in books or prizes, a new understanding. The surfeit of time taught her abundance.

People in wetsuits are surfing the Eisbach. As it passes under the bridge, the fast channel ploughs into a recess, creating a standing wave, information given to her by Amelia all those years ago as they finished ice creams melting over their hands. Amelia, placed beside Amal thanks to their closeness in the register. Amelia, with her confident stride and long blonde braid. Amelia, teaching her to paint, and receiving an education in photography by means of a trade. Amelia, hugging her at the airport and insisting she visit Vermont. Amelia, to whom she never spoke again. That's what people become: a collection of memories. Amal stands and watches the surfers jump off the bank and hover over the water.

Fresh sheets on the bed. New linen for her last night, a custom developed over time. The shutters on the balcony are open, allowing the summer air to come and go as it pleases. Amal imagines her older self wandering the streets of the city, heading nowhere in particular, greeting neighbours, deepening the lines which riddle her face and collect around her eyes, a reminder of each laugh, of each smile, of each happy day. Her body is thicker, ringed by time like an oak tree, a plentiful vigil.

In the morning, the bed sits blank, a page awaiting ink. Amal smooths the creases and stares at the emptiness. The suitcase lies open in the hallway. Clothes are folded in neat squares and weighed down with books. She checks under the bed, behind the sofa, in the fridge for any part of herself which has come loose and tucked itself away, desperate to stay. The apartment is bare and clear, a body fresh from the bath.

Airports are uncanny places. Entry points to cities bleached of all character. Amal sits by the long window and pecks at a sandwich purchased more for amusement than sustenance. Planes rattle along the runway and take off with a start as if lifted by the invisible hand of a child. The number for her gate is called, and she makes her way across the flat escalator. At security, she is passed a tray by the guard who repeats instructions over and over. She pictures herself a doll with its accessories laid out: sunglasses, belt and earrings, phone, passport, wallet, even her shoes.

The plane is half-empty and yet she has a neighbour. An eager Canadian using the aisle seat as a footrest as she shows Amal her phone, swiping through photo after photo of her travels - the same lone face in front of the Louvre, the Colosseum, the Brandenburg Gate. How lucky she is to take the trip, her cousin's wedding cancelled twice, her brother not allowed in for the birth of his first child, if only the government had acted like New Zealand. Amal tries her best to express interest from behind her mask: raises her eyebrows, cocks her head, gives a thumbs-up and feels ridiculous.

England, so sure of itself, hasn't changed. Piles of tourists disembark and wait for their luggage at the carousel, craning their necks as each case appears from the shoot, straining to see if they have lost the roulette. Flush with sun and wearing matching T-shirts, a group of men whoop as their bags arrive, slapping each other on the back and performing swaggering dances. Amal stands until the head of her case crowns.

A welcome silence clutches the train. She stares out as the country ticks by and looks at the evening sky latticed with soft clouds. The holiday is over, from tomorrow reality will resume. She opens her bag, retrieves the remaining sandwich (now a kind of souvenir) and chews to pass the time.

Before the pandemic, home meant freedom. The house liberated Amal, allowed her to sing, dance, eat spaghetti straight from the copper-bottomed pan. Free from having to put her best foot forward, from having to set an example, from having to praise, chastise, step in, mitigate, resolve, explain, respond, make her point clear. The virus changed matters. She found the front room invaded by litters of children peering at her through the screen and by anxious parents seeking reassurance that Tom, Iris, Charlie, Holly, Rojin wouldn't fall behind. How little she saw of the outside world, confined to the regular route of her run or an occasional coffee, all the while hoping she wouldn't bump into a mother or father demanding that she transform herself there and then, that she pause her shopping, that she lay down her first name and personality and attend to their every thought about handwriting, exams, the rugby league.

Left fallow, the flat has recaptured some of its old magic. The spell enters Amal as she leans against the door. In the kitchen, she lights incense and puts on the radio. A few hours until the languor dissipates, enjoyed slowly, the taste of coffee at the end of a meal. The crevices between her fingers are cracking again, so she takes a bottle of moisturiser from her bag and massages it across the skin, leaving the palms slick and cold. Replacing the bottle, she finds a round, white stone taken from the riverbank, holding it level against her hand to appreciate the fine grain, rubbing it between her fingers and generating pleasant warmth. An ordinary stone, gathered without a second thought, now bringing tears to her eyes, flowing, like the future yet to come.

The Gospel According to Penelope

To say I have an addiction is simply silly. An egregious exaggeration. Pure poppycock. Hysterical hyperbole. A true untruth – although it *is* stronger than a hobby. *Calling* captures it best. Or perhaps *A Passion*, though it shouldn't be confused with the Lord's. I could argue it's my duty, but don't feel the need. I was, however, compelled to correct Book Club Barbara when she droned on and on about my 'rabid obsession with shoes'.

'It's avid,' I said, then closed my book.

The poor dear can't help she garbles her words – many people do. Take the word *cobbler*. Everyone thinks cobblers make shoes. Not so. Cobblers *mend* shoes. *Cordwainers* make them. The distinction has been lost, confused into just one word. My father was a cobbler – so I know the difference, and I don't mix them – though it has to be said Father grew rather confused and garbled towards the end of his life.

Barbara's incorrect about *obsession* too – a word more appropriate for ill-smelling bottles of coarse scent. She babbles the word *addiction* too – which is better suited for unsavories like cigarettes, narcotics and internet S-E-X. It has no place describing an admiration of shoes. Never mind Barbara and that lot. I don't need Book Club to read books.

I won't be dissuaded from discussing footwear with anyone within earshot. And why should I? Shoes form a very natural part of everyone's daily life. I see no need to hide my collections or carry footwear guilt. And if I ever find out who decreed the collective noun for shoes *a scandal,* I'll denounce them forever.

I certainly meant it when I said, 'Shoe love is not a sin,' to Office Manager Michelle as she stood open-mouthed in front of the vast array I housed in a work cupboard. A shortage of space for her stationery supplies was hardly my concern. Of course I kept a few spare collections at work – there was no shame in that.

What was a shame was finding all my lovely shoes in a mound the next day, piled to overflowing on and around my desk – while her office stationery was all cupboard-tucked away.

I tried to enlighten HR Helen to my plight. Pled a most passionate case. Reminded her that, these days, it's good to be different. Diversity in the workplace is all the rage, even encouraged. By possessing a higher number of shoes than most, I was providing an opportunity to celebrate my diverse collection. I even offered to compromise. But my request for a two-metre tall, six-metre wide glass display case to store a small smattering of my office shoes was denied. I had no other choice but to resign. I recognised the futility in talking to a heathen.

The fact of the matter is that having extra shoes is proactive. Shows I'm planning ahead. As I told Gardener Graham, you never know when there's going to be a shoe emergency. And when it happens, I'm ready. There are, after all, four seasons – three-hundred and sixty-five days in a calendar year. No one with any footwear integrity would wear the same shoes for more than one season – unless, of course, the aforementioned shoe emergency had been declared.

Gardener Graham then mumbled something about needing to go mow the lawn – though he'd only mowed my small square yesterday. As he hurried away, I couldn't help but notice he was wearing the same tired pair of work boots he'd worn every single day. I'd seen him walking about town and in shops in these boots too. I suspected they were his only pair. I didn't take the decision lightly, letting him go. My rhododendrons and azaleas miss him. I softened the blow by telling him it was nothing personal, just a number of changes were afoot in my life. He took the news well, even seemed relieved.

I went on to confide to Shoe World Sheldon, my firm

footwear friend, that I'd resigned. Said it was the best decision I'd ever made. He proclaimed he would have done the same thing. We then concluded my second-best decision was buying a pair of purple velvet vintage Jimmy Choos at auction, sight unseen.

'Now you can fully follow your passion,' Shoe World Sheldon said, ringing up several new pairs of Siena suede sandals.

I suppose the obvious choice would have been to join the shoe-selling world, but it didn't seem like the right fit. As the daughter of a cobbler, I was destined for something different. Something greater. Something more. If I kept my footwear faith, life would reveal my footwear fate.

I believed this in part because I've always had a special relationship with shoes. A real connection. More than once I've walked past a skip when, suddenly, a tingle will start in my toes, rise to my head then extend to the ends of my limbs. I'll hear a sound like a strangled cry. Find it impossible to walk away. Begin digging through skip debris and discover perfectly good shoes discarded, abandoned simply because they needed a little TLC.

I'd always considered it simply a hobby, taking home shoes in this state. Often, they only needed reheeling, resoling and some dye on an unsavoury stain to be as good as new. I never dwelled on the abuse and neglect I'd seen. Instead, I focused on saving another pair as I hauled them out and fixed them up. Rejoiced when I could also salvage the box. Then I had a revelation… all these vast masses of shoes being cast aside, rejected, abandoned, they still had worth. They simply needed someone to rescue them. Heel them. Cleanse their soles. Give them a home. On the bus ride home from Shoe World, packages in both hands, I realised my true purpose: I'd become the Mother Theresa of shoes. Follow in Father's footsteps, but on a grander charitable scale and not worry about the finances.

You can always rely on shoes to put food on the table, Father liked to say. And they certainly did so – much more than Mother.

Of course, there would be sacrifices joining this saintly world. My shopping trips and friendship with Shoe World Sheldon would stop. I'd lose my loyalty discount. But I'd gain so many upcycled pairs of shoes. Like last week's chunky-heeled pair of Mary Jane's in black. It hardly mattered I already had twenty-seven similar pairs. There was such subtlety in black. Also, shoes rarely, if ever, disappoint me. Unlike people.

It gives me such great joy repairing and caring for rejected shoes. I feel real pride watching my collection grow. It doesn't really matter if my good shoe deeds aren't noticed, but sometimes, I imagine putting myself forward as the patron saint of shoes. Not that I want to step on anyone's toes. Heavens no! I have no complaints against the current incumbent – Blessed Theobald Roggeris. But occasionally I feel a bit more could be done. By someone with wardrobes and wardrobes of shoe-love to give. Like me.

This is no criticism of those at the top, in particular the one at the very top, holding the double honour of Patron Saint to Shoemakers and Foot Ailments: Saint Peter. He was quite right to balk when Jesus wanted to wash his feet. His trotters would have been ghastly from all that traipsing about the desert – after all, sandals are renowned for their inability to offer arch support and provide little protection from sun and sand. I, too, would have been embarrassed to have an A-lister like Jesus handling my tootsies without a proper wash and pedi first.

Thankfully, Peter saw the light. Received the message that clean feet equals clean living. Started his own foot-washing bonanza which, no doubt, gave him bonus points that helped him achieve his appointment as the first Pope. Once in the post, he remained loyal to the cause, watching over all things feet and feet-related. Quite cleverly, he extended his foot adoration into footwear. Gorgeous Papal shoes are not random chance. And I suppose it was while contemplating this fact I had my second revelation. People often say the Christian goal is to save souls. But I wondered if perhaps, over the years, the word *souls*, had become garbled – and that, originally, Christians were interested in saving *soles*.

It makes sense because, goodness knows, it's easier to mend shoes than people. Father would agree with this, though people need mending as well. They can be so cruel. I suspect Peter didn't suffer for his feet and shoe folly so why, I ask Neighbour Natalie, am I persecuted for my interest? I'm ridiculed, pointed at, receive endless eye-rolls and sighs as I try to spread the Good Word about insoles, shoe trees and negative heel technology. Neighbour Natalie never answers, just claims she urgently needs to walk her dog...although I've never seen her with one.

I'd love to chat with Saint Peter – I'm sure we'd have true rapport. I've often thought, as time goes on, how wonderful it would be to have someone with whom to discuss my shoe load. Some days I do feel the pinch. I'm not complaining. I know how to pack a corridor tight and don't mind sacrificing the corridors for wardrobes, although every now and again it would be nice to use the front door. I've got things sorted now with the postman. Delivery drivers all know to come round the back.

And while friends aren't as keen to visit anymore, fearing a tower-topple, that only happened once during one of Elsbeth's rare visits. My sister is a rather graceless klutz. It wasn't easy to remain calm as she shrieked, 'Christ on a bike, Penelope, you're a hoarding freak!'

I suppose she's envious of my life. Wasting hers looking for a man to fill Father's shoes, malingering and insisting she misses Mother after all this time. Two clear-cut cases of shoes being easier to mend than people. At least a large gin and tonic sooths after an Elsbeth session. She's sworn not to visit any more. Which is fine. We can meet out.

But to be honest, going out has lost its appeal – I don't like leaving my flock unattended. They really do provide much joy and folly. I now spend afternoons and evenings content in their captivating company. Whether it's taking a gorgeous pair of fuchsia mules for a satisfying lap between the lounge and the kitchen or strolling through the long grass in a pair of sparkling wellies, I'm positively spoilt for choice. Clicking around the kitchen table in red platform stilettos never loses its charm.

And yet, I confess that sometimes, when I'm sitting in the conservatory with a G&T, looking out onto the overgrown garden, I imagine Saint Peter appearing at my door. (He'll know to come 'round to the back'.)

Clad in his red leather Papal outdoor shoes and clutching one of those trendy man-bags, he'll appear just in time for pre-dinner drinks. After a light supper – I presume he still eats fish – we'll move outdoors for pedicures, recline on deck chairs to watch the sun set as our toes dry. Sip sweet sherry and put the world to rights. At some point, we'll move inside, and he'll slide into his indoor Episcopal sandals that he's tucked in his man-bag, while I slip into my red velvet kitten heels. We'll tango around the conservatory late into the night.

No doubt gossip will start when he stays. People will say he's moved his Papal slippers under my bed. But it won't be like that. In the *Gospel According to Penelope*, we'll be colleagues, complementing and complimenting each other on our parallel lines of work. I'll never be asked to choose between him and my shoes, and there'll be no worry of disappointment or heartache. We'll remain constant companions – after all, the best things in life come in pairs – spending the rest of our days side by side saving souls and soles.

Are We There Yet?

A former perfume factory in the middle of an orange grove, the song of the ocean, herbs underfoot, breakfast on a terrace drenched in sunshine, lush with jasmine and bougainvillea. So perfect on the website. Now all they needed were smiles for the camera.

She came to the terrace with a novel (detective fiction), her prescription sunglasses and a deep-brimmed hat for the sake of her freckles. He poured her some coffee; did his best to ignore the book. He was cutting his croissant into three neat territories – she noticed this; he'd replicated the map of the island. She tore hers in uneven shreds, smoothing butter over each ragged piece. They made plans for the day like a guerrilla leader and a general negotiating a ceasefire: great tension, superficial civility hiding a jangling mistrust, like both had Kalashnikovs stowed under the breakfast table, ready at any moment.

The hire car tacked between hill and coast; he behind the wheel, she almost wearing the map, an outsized origami project. Her planned itinerary: a pilgrimage into the imagination of her favourite crime writer, paying homage at the places that had inspired him, and then the film locations from the mini-series. His ideal trip: the best of the south's wineries along the cliff-top trail, hairpins a-plenty to showcase the famed vertiginous views - and his steering prowess. Later, he'd need a roadside pause to relinquish the driver's seat after another must-taste vintage nudged blood alcohol levels beyond the sensible. Insofar as he'd given any thought to their holiday, he'd pictured the impromptu – as far from team meetings at 11 as possible, and the al fresco - picnics, wine, sex. Siestas under a tree, the full peasant daydream.

Hope survived, these first two days, that by some voyager's voodoo they could splice their separate holiday wish-lists into one compatible tour. Striking out for a peninsular vineyard, the sat nav obliged *via points* that took in coastal switchbacks and also, seamlessly, the handsome municipality of Monte Grande, cinematographer's dream at the foot of an imposing bluff. Here, the sandstone town hall, with a few props, became the police station, inside which the Inspector's office scenes were filmed for such episodes as *The Owl's Call*, *The Tattoo Code*, and *Complicity of The Dunes.*

By day three, it was harder to find patience for yet another vineyard tour. Inevitable talk of the soil's limey qualities and of temperature control prefigured a dark passage through chill, echoing cellars, her teeth gritted, and familiar litanies of tannins, oaky notes and spiced berry. When, several blind alleys and a wild goose chase later, they arrived at the Inspector's beachfront apartment with most of the morning gone, he couldn't resist a mention of 'groupies' in reference to a small clutch of tourists already snapping and posing by the crime fighter's familiar veranda. The same tourists she would be joining in a few steps. She baulked at the word; a suspicion of sat nav foul play nagged in the back of her mind.

Back home, on non-holiday weeks, they were always busy - the cleaning, the shopping, the dinners for friends, work, study, bills. On holiday, there was so much time to fill, hours available for forensic analysis of each other's moods and motives, the frictions like pebbles rubbed together by the sea, and the spaces between. On the beach, the breakers bring back your thoughts, five times a minute. Bald truths and fossilised resentments tumble onto the shore. All those quirks, those cute, bewitching qualities that first caught your eye, like a sea-washed shell glinting in the sun, now washed up like flotsam.

Saltwater pool, encircled by orange trees: it was the detail on the website that most charmed her. She gazed a long time at those photos: glittering turquoise rhomboid lined with steamer chairs; imagined diving into its perfect blue, the bracing saline sting, a rush of bubbles over her skin. But the only thing she felt now, but a leg-length from that turquoise water, was creeping irritation. He rose and went to take a shower, turning the water on a bare trickle at first, cleansing every inch of wrists, forearms, then his neat shoulders, collarbones, neck. Removing all traces of sun cream in his fastidious way, without a drop of water wasted. The steel bracelet of his diver's watch flashed sunlight back at her, dazzling her eyes behind their Polaroid lenses.

She returned to the printed page, coloured shapes dancing between the lines for a time. Her Inspector was enduring a dark night of the soul. Under pressure from the Superintendent to close the case or give it over to a rival, he berated himself for being too slow to link clues, leaving townspeople vulnerable, for failing to outwit a people-trafficker and his sleazy lieutenants. She bit her lip - afraid, yet sure he'd do the right thing in a few more pages.

Earlier, they'd stopped for ice cream at a kiosk that had, rather brazenly, she thought, taken the Inspector's name. For a moment, chasing runnels of pistachio with her tongue, she saw herself as a groupie, someone's target audience, a gullible tourist ripe for cashing in. The kiosk drew her up short - the lines between fiction and reality blurred by some enterprising ice cream seller - it was okay to make your own fantasy - wasn't that what holidays were all about? But here was someone else manipulating reality for her, as if the Inspector was more than a fictional persona and actually did frequent the kiosk.

Her thoughts rewound now, searching for the moment when a figment of someone else's imagination became the hero in her life, supplanting the real flesh-and-blood man whose bunched back muscles were cutting channels up the saltwater pool now, churning blue to white. She watched his determined front crawl. Perhaps those feelings, those images of heroism that once filled her head, worked themselves loose after a while, with the jostling and bumps of everyday living. Perhaps she'd swept them up and locked them away in a drawer with other loose household things, mismatched buttons and washers, nails of obscure size, keys that fit no lock. Like the glamour and shine of photos from their wedding and first holidays, turned inwards - now, in the dark, silent folds of albums, those noble qualities were hidden from view. Thinking back to those heady days she felt a tiny burst of joy. The irritation ebbed from her, like the cool balm of lotion on sunburned skin. She looked back at the book in her hands.

A pale stripe where the sun hadn't tanned the skin: her ring, gone. She panicked, called him from the pool. He came: calm, concerned, water falling from all his angles. And like a true professional, he instigated a fingertip search of the dusty tracks between the orange groves, the grassy borders by the pool, the terrace, leaving no square foot un-inspected. She fretted and searched in the opposite direction, not nearly so methodical. The lost ring had left a cold, naked band on her, her hand felt stripped, vulnerable.

It was an hour, perhaps two, with the sun towering overhead, the hottest time of the afternoon and yet she felt shivery. She stood on a thorn, fell over a boulder, couldn't think straight in the heat. Her eyes on the pale dust, her toes in the grass; her mind was miles away, under the turquoise pool water, in the blue overhead. She was thinking of the mysteries of fiction: such addictive pleasure, so neat and contained, and why mysteries in real life were such messy, unravelled frustrations. The mysteries of communication, for example, why a man could never describe a person beyond passport-form check-box terms; why they could not name emotions or any colour beyond the primary spectrum. The mystery of what he saw in her, and of how he could be so self-contained yet need her reassurance so often as if her books were love rivals to be hated and suspected.

And, mysteriously, somewhere between the blades of grass and the shade cast by the orange trees, she began to pick up the trail again, a bloodhound with a fugitive's smell in her nostrils. The sense of intrigue that so often drew her nose into a book, now drawing her back towards her husband.

He came back briefly. 'Where did you last have it?' She realised she didn't know. It had become so much a part of her that she didn't notice it any more, like her pulse or her reading glasses. He stood beside her for a long time, looking along the terraces that ran in front of each apartment, and she could sense the deduction engines running overtime in his logical mind. In a sudden movement, he straightened up and walked directly to their terrace. A large blonde hound had claimed their patio for her daytime haunt from day one, after the neighbours shooed her away. Now she lifted her huge head and began lazily to beat her tail. Slowly, crouching in front of her, he smoothed the bear-like head. He turned to his wife. 'Weren't you playing with her this morning?'

'Um, yes.' She was almost sure, though here, the days seemed to blend into one; perhaps it had been yesterday? He had this knack, in some situations, of knowing her better than she knew herself. She may be in doubt, but he was certain.

He was already coaxing their adopted pet, gently, kindly. In a haze of lethargy, her black-rimmed eyes half-shut, the dog began to heave herself up, stretching her long limbs with great indulgence. Then, she seemed to think again and returned herself to the warm stone with a thud.

She watched her husband react. He didn't lose patience. She could see he was sort of charmed by the animal's indolence. He changed tactics and began to rub first a blonde flank and then her belly. The dog rolled onto her back, revealing two slabs of pink-gold sandstone. He smoothed his hand over the paving, running a finger between the mortar-joins, the other hand still on the dog. But there was no ring on the newly uncovered stone.

Watching the two of them, she remembered how his gentleness had surprised and beguiled her in the early days. Kindness, too, was a kind of heroism. She walked away a little, towards the orange groves, the fringe of green ocean beyond. A ring, perhaps, was not all that important. Material things, she told herself, we're all too attached to them: holiday thoughts. Turning, she looked back at her husband, now persuading the dog to roll onto her other side. And slowly, lazily, she was rolling, black eyes adoringly fixed on the face of the man offering so much attention as her head turned through 180°, paws flopping onto her chest. He leaned close into the ground, leg muscles straining. Something happened - she couldn't quite see - his shoulder moving - an odd horizontal rotation, forearm hidden behind the rise of the dog's ribcage. Her husband turned his head to her, arm still moving in the dog's shadow, then he rocked into an upright squat, took the dog's head in both hands and smoothed her ears. Now he walked towards her, stretching out a hand: in the palm, her ring.

They ate at their tiny table. The dog, enlivened by the cool night air, went off to prowl the orange groves. Filling his glass, she asked what he'd like to do tomorrow. He suggested the lake; she nodded. Her gaze dropped to her lap, admiring the ring, the way it caught the light. And from nowhere, the smell of paper in her nostrils, that rich, straw-like scent of words on pages, flipping over to a new chapter.

He went inside a little later to get his sweater and noticed her novel on the bench by their suitcases, a bookmark at the three-quarter point, roughly, abandoned under her beach bag.

Damn Lucky Sometimes

'You were fortunate to secure an appointment on such short notice,' the doctor said.

'Yes,' Kasia agreed respectfully. 'Damn lucky.'

'A patient of thirty years,' the doctor continued gravely, 'had her son call us three days ago to cancel her annual check-up. She suffered a debilitating stroke.'

That's in the head, right?' Kasia ventured. The son sounded intimidating. She could almost picture him, a busy man in another office – the head of a multinational company, perhaps. There were a lot of those nowadays in old Kraków's Market Square. They popped up like mushrooms. Do mushrooms have heads? she wondered. Or is it caps?

The doctor glanced at her from head to toe, and after sizing her up, he interjected, 'That's in the brain.'

'That's too bad,' Kasia offered sympathetically.

The doctor gave her an icy look.

'I mean no harm,' Kasia heard herself say all of a sudden, in a small voice.

The doctor's expert gaze, now alert, pierced her breast, and then slid to her womb.

'Please change into the gown,' he said, directing her toward a tall, slender screen.

Kasia disappeared behind it, undressed, and slipped into the garment that awaited her, neatly folded, on the stool. It was not the scratchy paper gown all the other doctors had laid out for her in the past, but an ivory, silky robe. She glanced in the mirror, closed her eyes, and felt again like a little girl, glued to the TV, watching the adventures of Princess Arabela, chased around by the evil wizard Rumburak, in Czech with Polish subtitles. Arabela (spelled with only one L on this side of the

Iron Curtain, so kids wouldn't get any pro-Western notions in their heads) would wear a white gown, a collar that was higher up the back of the neck than in the front, and a gold tiara, while the bearded Rumburak was clad in a dark-coloured mantle and a dangling silver medallion.

When she opened her eyes, the first thing she noticed was the framed diploma. Why was it hanging behind the screen and not above it? It spelled nothing out of the ordinary:

Jagellonian University
Founded 1364
Plus ratio quam vis

In town, everybody's diplomas – medical or not – read the same. Even Kasia, who didn't have one, knew what it meant. *Reason Trumps Force.*

'That's how we ended up with Auschwitz next door,' Polish students joked in cafés.

Auschwitz, or Oświęcim, was indeed a mere thirty miles away from Kraków. Kasia never went there – not even on a school trip. She'd worked full-time since her teens. Józef hadn't had a free day in ages either – until this summer, that is.

She emerged from behind the screen in a daze. She hadn't thought about Princess Arabela in years. Her childhood entertainment had consisted of cartoons featuring Bolek and Lolek; two ill-drawn boys who seemed to have gone bald before puberty, Mass thrice a week, and underground broadcasts of the Solidarity Movement.

'Do you experience any hot flushes?'

'A few,' Kasia grumbled.

'In that case, I'd expect you to reach menopause sooner than later. You're what, almost forty?' He leafed through the chart.

'Thirty-nine. I didn't know I was so close. So, a couple more years and it's over?'

'These things are not always set in stone, but most likely –

unfortunately – yes.'

'Phew.'

He pretended not to hear her.

'Thank God,' she insisted.

'Anything else bothering you?'

These doctors, they loved to change the subject. But she liked to get to the point.

'Doctor, I wonder, why does it take three days to get an appointment here?'

'Just making sure you're in good health, otherwise all our tests are free.'

That much was true. But those tests were a pain to sit through. In the waiting room, the minute she learned Kasia's blood type, the nurse became excited. All patients with that rare blood type – AB negative – qualified for additional screening this month, she had announced. It didn't cost extra. Actually, if Kasia submitted to those tests, they'd waive the OB/GYN fee. Of course, as with all clinical studies, Kasia wasn't being forced to enroll, but why on earth wouldn't she?

So, three free hospital lunches and a bunch of gibberish called 'immune markers' later, here she stood, dressed like Princess Arabela.

'Do you like the gown?' the doctor smiled benevolently.

'Yes. It's real silk. It's been years since I've seen anything like this.'

'You can keep it when we're done.'

The breast examination was the easiest she'd ever had. He uncovered only a bit at a time, and palpated gently, but deftly. *How considerate*, she thought.

'Now don't be alarmed. I have to strike your back with my fist. Right side first.'

'I've never had a doctor do that to me before.'

'Maybe you don't have the best doctor, then.'

'What's it for?'

'To rule out kidney disease.'

'My husband passed a stone on the kitchen floor once. It

wasn't pretty. Turned out it runs in the family – some kind of kidney trouble or the other. You name it, they had it.'

In his family? Not on your side of the family. That's what you wrote on the form.'

'Yes. I was just thinking about my children.'

'That's understandable. Does it hurt here?' – and he gave her the sharpest nudge in the corner between her ribs and spine she didn't know existed, so deeply was it hidden.

'Nah. I did feel a tickle, though.'

'That's normal. How about here, on the left?'

'Even less.'

'Perfectly normal.'

'You win.'

'I didn't win anything yet,' the doctor smiled. Why couldn't she help but think he looked like Rumburak?

'Lie back for the pelvic examination, please.'

He was thin, old, and dignified. He sported a pince-nez and a goatee. She glanced at him one more time, then slid back.

'You're a magician,' Kasia rubbed her eyes once he was done. 'I didn't feel a thing.'

'I'm glad you didn't feel a thing. This tiny thing inside you, however, feels everything. I can't help you hurt it, no more than I would ever hurt you,' the doctor said. He turned his back on her, went to the sink, took his gloves off, and emphatically washed his hands of the whole affair.

Just like the others. But this was Poland, after all, so something had to give.

A great silence followed. He motioned her to get dressed and pretended to bury himself in a medical tome, while she started dressing and pretended to get lost in her buttons and zippers.

Something was in the air. She could sense it. This was her lucky day.

'I can't help you,' the doctor said, closing his book with a snap, but instead of ringing for the nurse he said, 'unless you help me.'

This was it. This she knew how to play along. She had to stay calm and play cool.

She still wore her modest engagement ring next to her wedding band – a joke of a ring Józef had given her in tenth grade. She flashed it at him, the way Arabela used to point her enchanted ring at Rumburak, twisting it around her finger to turn the magician into a toad or a goat, and smiled seductively. 'I don't have that kind of money.'

'Neither God nor man can help you,' the doctor told Kasia, who had slumped back on the examination table, demure and half-dressed, 'unless you help yourself. This is Poland, after all.'

The window was open, so she took in the breeze and the linden tree fragrance instead. A violin was screeching somewhere below, right between her legs. The old doctor rented an office in a reputable establishment, filled with conservative students and lawyers and a day care on the ground floor – and she thought of Zosia at home. Little Zosia, home alone. Well, not so little anymore: fourteen, ready for her confirmation ceremony, and supposed to be practising the piano for an hour a day, except she never seems ready for that chore. Would Jan be keeping an eye on her as he'd promised? Forget it. All that boy has on his mind is football. It didn't matter; Bronia'll tell on both of them, breathlessly, as soon as Kasia walks in the door tonight.

Three children at home, and nothing ever the same since her husband left; he'd gone to buy cigarettes and never returned. The last she'd heard of Józef, he was in America in search of a brighter future. To be fair, he'd removed nothing from their home except his carpenter toolbox.

If only he'd taken Jan along; she'd heard they handed out athletics scholarships over there like crazy. That's all Kasia would have suggested, had she been consulted. But, as even her own mother would say, why ask Kasia, she's not that bright; just damn lucky sometimes.

'This consultation is over. I can't help you,' the doctor said to Kasia for a third time, gentler, her legs half spread, 'because this is Catholic Poland. I don't want to lose my license or go to jail for you. But I can help you save one life while you take another, so you won't go to hell. We'll both go to purgatory instead. Give the gift of life, Kasia. Don't sit on it.'

Kasia, still perched on the examination table, perked up. This one doctor hadn't urged her to save a soul, but a life. He might just have a plan. She made the sign of the cross on the dry roof of her mouth with her tongue so she'd remember to hold it. Damn lucky. Damn lucky sometimes.

'I have a daughter your age. It's hard bringing up kids.'

Kasia nodded, teary-eyed, feigning relief.

His voice trailed off as he pointed to some fashion icon pictured skiing in Austria on the cover of a glossy magazine on his antique desk. She was so elegant she upstaged the classiest set-up.

'My husband,' Kasia replied stupidly, 'was a carpenter. I can get you finer furniture.'

'Blonde, green-eyed, just like you,' the doctor interrupted her impatiently, with a wave of the hand. 'The two of you could be twins. Same blood type, same skin glow. You could have easily landed the same photo shoots, the same chances in life. Unfortunately she can't...'

He stopped short, choking with emotion. Now that he'd moved out of the way, Kasia saw there was something unhealthy about his daughter's rosy cheekbones and gorgeous tan: a skillfully made-up mask covering an ashen face. She'd seen that face before – on her mother-in-law's body, hooked to a dialysis machine amidst a sea of ashen faces; not grey, like the Poland she'd grown up in, but ashen like she imagined Auschwitz would have been: the resigned, official stamp of death. This girl's eyes were already sunken. She didn't have much time left.

Neither did Kasia. Her lunch break was almost over. But had the doctor bought into her dumb act, after all? It looked like she was close now – so close the room started spinning around her, and the doctor's voice sounded farther away than she knew it to be, now flooding the examination room, now pulling away, tide-like. She felt invisible, like the fly on the wall the fairy Princess Arabela turned herself into when her fiancé Petr took exams, so she'd be able to buzz the answers into his ear – Arabela, who had descended in the guise of an ordinary girl into the world of commoners to escape Rumburak. She'd better hold it together, she'd better not lose it – she just had to get rid of it, this thing inside her that she'd been trying to get rid of, or trade off, for months.

'I'll take care of it all myself,' the doctor whispered. 'Nobody needs to know.'

'I can sue you,' Kasia replied faintly.

'You've got me wrong. Mary's not interested in your baby any more than you are. You two are in that respect, as in all others, a perfect match.'

And thus, some two thousand years after the birth of Christ, Kasia Kaszinska gave up a kidney in exchange for an abortion.

El Scorcho

Memory and I disagree on what to preserve. I treasure the mundane, the entitled grasp of a toddler's doughy hand, or the sight of a loved one in the disembarking crowd at an arrivals gate. She doesn't save these modest moments.

It is not an issue of capability. She provides crystal-edged simulations of her preferred material.

One of her favourites, I know as *El Scorcho*, and those two words, which were meaningless to me at the time, dissolve the decades since, galvanizing the memory of that half hour in a rental car, into my present.

The windows are open to the relentless midday heat of a Florida summer's day, and the sun beats down on us unchecked. My sister and I sit on opposite sides of the flesh-toned bench seat, three and a half years obscuring the inches between us. At any moment, one of us is on the shaded side of the car, against the door, face thrust out into the torpid breeze, while the other is shrinking away from her window to avoid the swath of sun and scorching vinyl.

Each is lost in her hopes: the one in the shade hoping that the car continues straight, allowing her more time on the cooler side; the other staring straight ahead onto the road ahead, hoping that the car will turn, and the sun will shift to her sister's half.

Right now, I am the one hiding from the sun. I sit upright and still, feet flat on the floor, perching on the edge of the bench, just far enough back to keep my shorts fabric between my leg and the seat, trying not to let skin touch vinyl.

Stay alert! Losing your balance costs you, and turns come quickly and without warning, like riding a roller coaster blindfolded. Sharp left turn, fall onto my sister, heads and shoulders collide. Sharp right turn, a cheek or worse, lips, branded by metal window trim. Either way, a muffled squeak before bolting erect again.

We are silent.

My sister's thin T-shirt and shorts hang lank on her little body, her corn-silk crown is dark, fused to her pale forehead, and her face is flushed along her cheeks and nose as if she is stained from having her head dunked into a pink-frosted birthday cake.

I must look the same. I feel the beads of sweat squeezing out of creases, chasing one another into rivulets, racing down to flash flood my underwear. I am sitting in a squishy warm pool, like I have just peed myself. Maybe I have. We have been driving since breakfast.

The car rolls to a stop.

I watch the waves of heat swelling beyond the hood, blurring the other cars. The acrid fumes of pavement and exhaust bleed into the car, soiling the air. I blink and swallow to flush the sting as I look up at the light. I can feel my sister's gaze on it as well, willing it to turn green.

And then, it does. The car starts moving. The air starts moving. We can breathe again. Have I been holding my breath? We shift our sights, separate again, and she leans out, out into the air on her side.

After a minute, I feel the relief of the current against my sticky skin and my breathing slows.

My father's head rises above the wall of the front seat, a slick black half-moon looming above me. I cannot see my mother. She is sunken in her seat, somewhere in front of my sister. My father turns regularly to the right, checking on her, so I know she is still there.

Our father is driving, talking – to us, to himself, to our mother. We don't know, and no one responds. No matter, he keeps talking.

Our mother is mute. If I stretch forward and peer over the

top of the seat, I can see her, folded in on herself, staring into the middle distance, entranced by something else, outside the burning car.

I follow her gaze. It is mesmerising, this peculiar flat place, with its needle-straight streets lined with squat, faded buildings, one after another on patch-worked paved lots. So different from our cool tree-shadowed roads at home, winding up and down leafy green hills.

'Who wants to eat?' my father asks. No one answers.

'Marcella?' That is me. Named for my father's mother, of whom my father speaks with his church voice.

I didn't spend much time with her. Memory's portrait depicts her staring down at me with her owl eyes from behind pointy glasses, pressing her thin pale lips together. Her arms are rigid against her sides as if to make sure she won't mistakenly touch me.

She had been called Rita. My father never allowed me a nickname. He strictly forbade it, saying it would be an insult to his mother. I don't understand, but I don't ask about it anymore.

'Marcella?' I hate my name, and I hate that I was named after her. 'Do you want to eat?'

The car suddenly swings to the left and I fall into my sister. When we right ourselves, I see we are next to a large board with pictures of food and soft drinks tinkling with ice. Some of the words have flames next to them. I look back at my sister and she is staring out my window; I see beads of sweat perched above her lip. She could use a Coke too, but she doesn't say anything. She just stares.

'Look! They have all sorts of tacos here. You can pick your sauce.' His voice rises with delight. He seems excited about the sauce situation.

'Mild, Medium, Hot, Very Hot and El Scorcho!' Super excited now.

'Marcella. Wanna bet?' My stomach makes a fist.

My father loves contests. No, that's incorrect. He loves to best others, and he does this by regularly challenging people to meaningless stunts.

'Marcella,' he repeats. 'I bet I can eat a taco with El Scorcho sauce and you can't.'

Reflexively, I open my mouth to speak. 'I can.'

I don't know why I say it. I have never had a taco before. Ever. I am not even sure what a taco is. I have only ever heard the word taco on TV. I don't even like spicy food.

'OK! We'll see who wins!' Nothing excites my father as much as the anticipation of beating someone else at something. It doesn't matter what, or who his opponent is. The only thing that matters is winning.

I don't listen as he places the order. I don't hear whether or what the other two in the car order.

The next thing I know I am holding a hot, dripping handful of warm, wet, ground meat in a wilting shell, and fumes of spiced heat are shooting up my nose. I want to throw it out the window, but I don't dare. I force myself to take a bite. I have to. I know this game. I stupidly agreed to it, and now I have to finish it out, or risk teasing, or worse, anger.

I know the second that my lips touch it that I am doomed. It is fire. It scalds my lips and tongue and burns the skin off the top of my mouth before slipping down my throat like molten lava. I want to howl in pain, but I don't.

My father crunches away on his taco.

'This is great!' Even through the pain, I can hear the laughter in his voice.

How can he be enjoying it, I wonder as tears flood my eyes?

I choke down bite by bite, taking huge gulps of air in between to cool my burning mouth and throat. I am only able to breathe through my mouth now. My nose is running from the heat of the spices, running into my bites of food, but I don't care. I keep jamming it into my mouth until there is nothing left in my hand but a greasy paper wrapper. My hands, arms and thighs are streaked with spicy sauce, and my skin is tingling from it, but I have no napkin to wipe myself. It is OK though, because I have finished it. I have done it. The worst is over.

I notice that the car is moving again. I don't have any idea of how long it took me to eat it.

'Did you finish it?' From the tone, I know that this is a repeated question, and I must answer.

'Yes,' I croak as I scoot into the scorching rectangle of sun-soaked vinyl next to the window to reach the air outside. The burning in my mouth and throat is increasing by the second. I press up against the sizzling trim of the baking door, oblivious to the pain from my exposed skin. I open my mouth and steer my face into the wind to try to cool my insides.

I had finished my soda a few bites into the taco and have nothing else to drink. Swallowing seems to make the burning pain worse, so I just hold my mouth open. I am on fire - my heart is racing, sweat is pouring out of me, and the heat inside me seems to be increasing instead of decreasing. I can't think of anything besides the excruciating pain screaming from my lips too deep in my throat.

He is talking, so I try to focus. 'Well, I finished mine too.' I am confused by the glee in his voice. I don't understand, but I can't concentrate enough to figure out what I'm missing.

'OK,' I rasp. It hurts to speak. My mind wanders out of the car, away from the pain, leaving my little girl body behind, mouth and eyes wide in perpetual shock, like a mounted trophy fish.

'Guess what? GUESS WHAT?!'

I force myself back into the car.

'MARCELLA! Guess what?!' I can hear his toothy grin.

He doesn't wait for me to answer. He starts laughing, his peculiar machine-gun cackle. 'Hee, hee, hee!'

He is choking on his mirth and can barely squeeze out his punchline. 'My taco had regular sauce! Yours had El Scorcho - and mine had regular! Hee, hee, hee, hee!'

The car is silent but for his giggling. I don't look at my mother or sister. They are not there. I felt them recoil into themselves at 'wanna bet.' I wish I could have too.

I hoist my shoulder up onto the edge of the door to lean out again, farther this time. I don't feel the hot metal against the pale skin of my underarm. I only feel the fire inside of me. I face forward, my sauced-stained mouth wide open to the wind in a silent scream, as streams of tears streak back into my hair.

I remain there in the eternity of memory.

The Authors

Clare Reddaway - The Stoat (p1)
Bath-based writer Clare Reddaway's stories have been out and about in the world. Recent highlights include being long-listed (top 50) for the *BBC National Short Story Award*, shortlisted for the *Bridport Prize* and publication of standalone short, 'The Guts of a Mackerel' by *Fly on the Wall Press.*

Ruth Edwardson - Don't Forget Your Dancing Shoes (p6)
Ruth lives in Essex. She mulls over ideas for stories while walking and watching wildlife. She has been published in independent magazines, such as *Scribble*, and shortlisted in competitions including, *Writers' Forum.* This is the first time being shortlisted means being published too. She loves Parracombe!

Kenneth Pimentel - Karth8 (p12)
Ken Pimentel is a writer, tech geek and sailor. Raised in California, Nigeria, and England, he now lives in France with his wife and daughter. In 1994, he co-authored a book on virtual reality and continues to work in the field at *Epic Games.* Karth8 is his first contest submission.

Martin Phillips- All the Things You Aren't (p16)
Martin Phillips was an English teacher and English adviser but now devotes his time to writing. He won first prize at the *2020 Yeovil International Literary Festival* and second prize in the *Anansi Archive* competition in 2022. He was longlisted for the prestigious *Bridport Short Story Competition* in 2021.

Hilary Orme - The Yellow Man (p22)
Following a long career in education, Hilary Orme began writing to raise funds for Macmillan Cancer Support. To date, she has published four children's books and a collection of poetry, recently featured on the BBC. She is currently working on a historical novel about the poet Richard Lovelace.

Valerie Bowes - Playing Safe (p28)
I've always loved writing. When I was no longer needed to drive a truck around the building sites of London, I was free to put my words down on paper, instead of doing it in my head while negotiating traffic. My website is valeriebowes.com

Leks Drakos - Here is my Heart (p35)
Dr Leks Drakos is a rogue academic (vivat humanitatis!), monsterologist, and reluctant marketing shill. He specialises in researching and writing about the end of the world. leksikality.com or tweet @leksikality

Gladys Chudley - The Knife (p49)
Gladys Chudley writes for pleasure and is delighted to have a story published in *Parracombe Prize 2022*. Gladys' favourite book series is *Thursday Next* (a character she secretly wishes to be). Gladys enjoys swimming in the sea and spending time with family and friends - and she loves her dog.

Rosa Chalfen - Nicki (p42)
Rosa is a final year English student at the University of Oxford. Next year, she is studying an MA in Creative Writing at the University of East Anglia. Her writing has been published in various magazines, and she was shortlisted for the *Streetcake Experimental Writing Award* 2019 and 2021.

Tom O'Malley - Love in Paris (p48)
A guidebook writer living in St Leonards-on-sea, Thomas likes stories that involve travel, history and speculative realities.

Maureen Cullen - It Would Take a Miracle (p53)
Maureen lives in Argyll and Bute. In 2015, she was awarded an MA in Creative Writing from Lancaster University. She has stories and poems published in a range of magazines. In 2021, Maureen was shortlisted for the *V. S. Pritchett Short Story Prize*. Maureen can be found on Twitter @maureengcullen

Rishika S – Unshackled (p59)
Rishika is an aspiring author who has spent years ghost-writing everything from non-fiction to fantasy. She has most recently been working on her own three-book series - a character-driven historical fiction - while juggling her day job as a marketer and working on her book review blog.

Thomas Smith – Faithful (p66)
Thomas Paul Smith is a writer from London, England. He currently works as a radio producer in Dubai, UAE. His work has appeared in *Bridge Eight, Paranoid Tree* and *404 ink*.

Gerry Webber - The Misbegotten (p72)
Gerry Webber lives in Edinburgh where he is a member of the Stobie Stories writing group. He has published a number of short stories, most recently in the *Iron Press 'Aliens'* collection (2021) and continues to write for pleasure.

Richard Hooton - Hunger (p78)
Richard Hooton was born and brought up in Mansfield, Nottinghamshire and studied English Literature at the University of Wolverhampton before becoming a journalist and communications officer. He has had numerous short

stories published and has won or been listed in various competitions. Richard lives in Mossley, near Manchester.

Alexandra Gough - The Goose Thief (p86)
Alexandra Gough is a writer and translator from Surrey. She was shortlisted for the *Exeter Short Story Prize* in 2018 and came second in the 2021 *John Dryden Literary Translation* competition. Most recently, she made the 2022 *Wolverhampton Literature Festival* poetry prize shortlist. She is currently working on a novel.

Dean Gessie – Transitioning (p93)
Dean Gessie is an author and poet who has won dozens of international awards and prizes. Recently, Dean won the *Aesthetica Creative Writing Award* in England, the *Allingham Arts Festival Poetry Competition* in Ireland, the *UN-aligned Poetry Contest* in Finland and a *Creators of Justice Literary Award* in New York.

Gregor McKinlay - The Despised (p97)
I grew up in Australia and now live in Scotland. My writing is largely based around life experiences or historical fantasy. My love of nature tends to weave itself into my stories.

KA Bigelow – Porch Light (p103) and Many Happy Returns (p169)
I have written more than a hundred short stories and was recently named a finalist for the Saturday Evening Post's *Great American Fiction Contest.* I have always believed and taught that story and humour are fundamental human traits (like hiccups).

Wendy Swarbrick - Gnawing Worries (p108)
Wendy is a retired Physics teacher living in Sussex. Sometimes, between garden, spaniel, house and husband, she finds time to write. Find her books at www.knightgardebooks.uk

Dan Micklethwaite - Troglodyte Redux (p115)
Dan writes a wide range of stories in a shed in the north of England, and his debut novel, 'The Less than Perfect Legend of Donna Creosote,' was published by *Bluemoose Books*. Follow him on twitter @Dan_M_writer and visit danmicklethwaite.co.uk for more information.

Anil Classen - The Seven Year Itch (p119)
Anil, born in South Africa, exchanged the hustle of Hamburg for sheep-grazing Switzerland which proved to provide enough inspiration to keep his writing alive. His short story explores the relationship of culinary obsession, something that always surprises and delights. After all, what is more universal than a plate of food?

Emma Ayteen - Dear Neighbour (p125)
Emma was given a writing course as an unexpected present from a friend, wanting to give her something constructive to do during a) lockdown, b) self isolation, and c) whilst recovering from a broken wrist and ankle. This is Emma's second feasible attempt at a short story.

Alison Allen - Growing Power (p133)
A former teacher, Alison Allen now writes full time. Her stories have been published online by *Fictionjunkie, Café Lit* and *ShortKidStories,* and she has also had success in poetry competitions. When not working on her YA novel-in-progress, Alison enjoys volunteering with the Surrey Wildlife Trust.

Jean Hyland – Migrants (p139)
I am a third generation New Zealander. On the family tree are ancestors from both Lancashire and Devon. For many a year, acting and teaching provided a living. These days, the focus of

my work is writing. My book, 'Voice to My Suffering (a life history of Bickleen Ng Wang)', was published in 1999.

Peter Dunn - No Stomach For It (p145)
I grew up on a council estate in Liverpool, became a Ford apprentice, then 'ran away' to Germany with a rock band. I later studied art which blessed me with a living. I write compulsively. I am seeking publication for two novels – 'Brunelleschi's Quest' and 'Masaccio is Missing'. www.arte-ofchange.com.

Ros Levenson - Too Much Information (p151)
Rather late in life, as retirement loomed and lockdown began, Ros Levenson turned to creative writing and found that she loved it. She is now an enthusiastic writer of short stories and is studying for an MA in Creative Writing at the University of Hull. Ros lives in London.

Chris Cottom - DIY Derek (p156) and Veedon Fleece (p160)
Chris Cottom won the *2021 Retreat West Flash Fiction Prize* and was the People's Choice Winner of the *LoveReading Very Short Story Award 2022*. His stories appear, or are forthcoming, in anthologies by the *Bournemouth Writing Prize, Cranked Anvil*, and *Retreat West*, and have been broadcast on BBC Radio Leeds.

Tim Hatton - The Last Trip to See Ernest (p163)
Tim Hatton was born and raised in a mining and textiles town in North Nottinghamshire, shortly before the pits and factories were all closed. He enjoys writing stories with humour and pathos about the characters who inhabited this world, which seems long gone but remains seared into his memory.

Tadhg McCullough - August (p176)
Tadhg McCullough is a teacher and writer who lives in

London, near the park where men go cruising. Most recently, he was shortlisted for the *Grindstone Literary Prize* and the *Val Wood Prize.*

Sherry Morris - The Gospel According to Penelope (p182)
Originally from Missouri, Sherry Morris (@Uksherka) writes prize-winning fiction from a farm in the Scottish Highlands where she pets cows, watches clouds and dabbles in photography. Her first published story was about her Peace Corps experience in Ukraine. Visit www.uksherka.com for more of her published work.

Fiona Thackeray - Are We There Yet? (p188)
Fiona Thackeray's corona-chronicle made the *2021 BBC National Short Story Awards* longlist. Other good writing days include winning *The Macallan/Scotland on Sunday* and *Happenstance* prizes, being broadcast on BBC R4 and longlistings in the *Edge Hill University* and *Frank O'Connor Prizes.* She's working on a novel about a circus fire.

Sultana Banulescu - Damn Lucky Sometimes (p194)
Sultana Banulescu holds an MFA in Creative Writing from New York University and a PhD in History from the City University of New York. Sultana's fiction was awarded the *Gulf Coast Prize*, the *Katherine Anne Porter Prize*, and other distinctions. She is working on her first novel.

Marcella Hourihane - El Scorcho (p201)
Marcella Hourihane studied English at Dartmouth College and then Law at the University of Connecticut. She loves a good story and a laugh. She always wanted to be a writer, and now she is. She has three adult children and lives in Connecticut with her husband and dogs.

Printed in Great Britain
by Amazon

82086583R00129